Happy Sherlocking :)

Amy Dupire

god-thing

and other
weird & worrisome tales

Amy Dupire

Pamplemousse Publishing | Madison, Wisconsin

Pamplemousse Publishing
Madison, Wisconsin
www.authoramydupire.com

Cover and interior art by Grace A. Griffin

Book Layout © 2014 BookDesignTemplates.com

All Kinds of Hell/Amy Dupire. -- 1st ed.
ISBN 978-0-9904929-1-7

With immeasurable gratitude to my dearest Phil, for many happy years of marriage and lots of breakfasts.

And with somewhat less gratitude to Joss Whedon and Neil Gaiman, for many happy hours of entertainment and no breakfast.

CONTENTS

The Fortune Teller

Madame Lamar

Palmistry and Fortune Telling

The words were black and bold against the salmon pink background. The sign itself was in the shape of a hand, palm out, as if to say, "Don't even think about coming in here."

Maura took a deep breath and looked both ways before dashing up the sidewalk toward the door of Madame Lamar's house. Her heart thumped in her throat, making her feel slightly queasy. If anyone were to see her here. . . . Maura shuddered and took another quick glance around.

She shielded herself from street view in an overgrown spirea bush that encroached on the porch, and rapped on the door with her knuckles. Seconds slid away as she strained her ears for the sound of footfalls. Her mouth went dry. One more knock and Maura was preparing to run back to the sidewalk when the door rattled and swung inward.

Maura blinked, half-bewildered by the woman inside. She was tall and lean, in her early thirties, with short, black hair in tight African spirals. She wore spandex shorts, a tank top, and purple tennis shoes. Maura, who had rather expected sweeping skirts and gold disk earrings, was slightly taken aback.

"Girl Scout Cookies already?" the woman said. Her voice was loud but not unfriendly. "What are they, ten dollars a box this year?" She laughed and gave a feral smile revealing white, even teeth.

"No, ma'am. I-I'm looking for Madame Lamar."

"Well, you've found her! Come on in." The woman swept Maura—not one moment too soon—into a dark paneled entry. "Are you here on business or are you doing a paper for school? No, wait. Don't tell me!" The woman's eyes raked her up and down, and she nodded. "Business, definitely. You've got a serious look about you."

"Yes, ma'am. I guess you could say tha—"

"Good lord! There's no reason to keep 'ma'am'ing me. Frances is fine, or Ms. Lamar—you know, if you want to keep it professional. I prefer Frances." She laughed again and strode down the hallway, clearly meaning for Maura to follow. They slipped through a doorway hanging with strings of silver beads that clicked and hissed at their passing. The feel of them brushing along her body made Maura's flesh creep.

"Sit, sit," Frances directed her, and Maura lowered herself into a blue upholstered chair while the woman darted around the room like a dragonfly, first lighting candles then cutting the sunlight sliding through the blinds. They shut with a snap, and the warm glow of the flames swelled, casting odd shadows on the walls and floor. Frances took a half-dozen large rings from a glass bowl on a side table and slid them onto her fingers.

"What's your name, hon?"

"It's. . .Rebecca," said Maura.

"Rebecca. Very nice! Well, I was just headed to Pilates, Rebecca, but I can catch the spinning class later. It's always a treat to have a young person come see me. So much to read. So many big things ahead for you! Here, you look thirsty."

She poured a glass of water from a bottle in a mini-fridge and handed it to Maura before alighting in a chair across from her.

"Now, let's see," Frances began. "A girl like you—you look so smart—you can't be here because you're worried about school." Maura kept quiet, giving nothing away. "Family, is it? The teens are hard. Let me guess, you're fifteen? Sixteen?"

"Sixteen," lied Maura.

"Hard time with your parents? Divorced?"

"Yes," Maura admitted.

"You're living with. . . your Dad. That's a bit unusual."

Maura started at this and took a sip of water to wet her mouth before she could respond.

"My mom. . . left. She didn't even tell me she was going, just left."

Frances nodded sympathetically. "I'm so sorry. You have a step-mom?" she said slowly. Then she frowned, understanding. "Step-*moms*?"

Maura shrugged. "Not moms, just steps. Someone new all the time."

"The last one was mean," Frances suggested gently.

So is my dad, Maura thought, but she said merely, "I can take care of myself." She sat up straighter in the chair, steeling herself. It was getting too personal now. Maura knew the woman had the gift, but this was still something of a shock. "I just hate not knowing what's going to happen next," she confessed. "I don't want to be surprised any more. I want to see everything coming, clear as day."

"I'm sorry, hon. That stinks." Frances reached across and patted her with a warm hand. "Maybe we can help you out a little bit. Give you some courage for the future, huh?"

"Yes, *please*. That's what I want more than anything." Maura checked herself. She didn't want to sound overeager.

"Well, we could read a Tarot spread for you, or just take a look at your hand."

"Actually—"

"And I don't want you to worry about how much it's going to cost," said Frances, raising her hand along with her voice to ward off Maura's presumed question. "Especially the first time—not for young people. Generally I just ask for a symbolic payment. A quarter, or dime, or nickel. Whatever. The 'cross-my-palm-with-silver' formality is a tradition with me." Francis gave her a wink.

Maura passed over a quarter with a trembling hand which, once emptied, she wiped on her shorts.

"There's no reason to be nervous, hon. What's the matter?"

"Well, I was just w-wondering," Maura cleared her throat and started again, "How can you see the future? I mean, how did you get your gift?"

The fortune teller smiled, used to this line of questioning. "Well, when I was younger, I learned I was good at reading people. The way they sat or worked their hands or cocked their heads told me a lot. And if I'd calm myself a little, I could actually understand a bit of what was inside of them. *Feel* the things that were showing on the outside. And sometimes I'd get a glimpse of what was ahead of them, too."

Maura nodded and traced a line in the condensation gathering on her water glass. "I've heard that some people are like. . . psychic vampires, sort of. Stealing other people's gifts to strengthen their own. Sucking their ability right out of them. Disabling them." Maura watched the water coalesce under her finger and streak down the glass. She couldn't meet Frances's eyes.

"You've been watching too much cable," the woman said dryly. "Is that what you think I've done? Because I promise you I've never been a. . ." she grimaced, "'psychic vampire.' It sounds horrible."

"It is. It's a horrible, horrible thing."

"Well, I promise my seeing has nothing to do with hurting people." Frances regarded Maura with a gentle expression. "Are you sure you want to do this? You don't have to."

"I do. I *do* have to." Maura sighed, dried her palms again on her shorts, and seized one of the Frances's hands in her own.

"You're in terrible danger," Maura said.

Frances's smile stiffened. "Are you being funny? Isn't that supposed to be my line?"

"I'm not being funny. Something bad is going to happen to you. And I'm really, *really* sorry."

Frances didn't look scared yet, merely hurt. But that soon changed.

"I have to know what's going to happen next for *myself*," insisted Maura. "I can't take the waiting."

Frances's hand twitched in Maura's, but the rest of her was frozen still. Her eyes were fixed, staring without seeing. Maura raised the woman's wrist to her forehead and knelt at her feet. She could feel the blood pulsing in the vein there. Taste the scent of her skin.

Frances was immobile as a stone angel and just as silent, save for her raspy panting.

A faint mist began creeping in on the edges of Maura's vision, and suddenly she could see into Frances' mind, into the myriad of jumbled visions housed there in layers and fragments. A painful electricity raced through Maura and she gritted her teeth against the onslaught. One moment, she could see herself through Frances' eyes, and immediately that image was overshadowed by another—of Frances looking at herself in the mirror and patting her face. She was blank, frightened, unsure of even her own body.

Maura felt a pang of guilt. Frances would never "see" after this. And she'd never be quite herself—but at least she'd live. She would come out better than the last fortune teller had.

Flashes of memory (*of future memories?*) flitted through Maura's mind: golden leaves trembling in the breeze, a man's head thrown back in laughter, the interior of a cluttered car, a pink tiled shower. Faster and faster they came, until the former Madame Lamar slumped in her chair.

Maura looked up to see the lids slide shut over Frances's walnut-brown eyes. She was unconscious still, but her breathing had steadied.

Maura rose on trembling legs. She picked up her water glass and wiped away the fingerprints on her shirt. As she did, her vision swam, and another scene came to view.

Ah, yes. . . *yes*. She would get away with this. She could *see* it. But other things were still too fuzzy. It was improvement, at least.

She blew out the candles, softly, so as not to splatter the wax before stealing out the back door. There, she paused to finger a fading primrose, and several of the pink petals fluttered to the porch.

"I'm sorry," she said.

As she breezed away from the house, another image flashed in Maura's head—her father in the living room with a case of Miller and the TV on too loud. He stood uneasily, one hand on his chair looking up at the clock. His gaze dropped to the front door, his eyes narrowed, and the muscle in his jaw twitched.

She had seen that before—and told herself she'd never see it again.

Maura had made her decision before she reached the intersection. She turned left, instead of right, and kept on going.

Wake

I try not to get attached to the people around me—not because I'm cold-hearted, but because they don't really exist. They're all going to disappear as soon as I can wake up.

I'm not certain how long I've been sleeping. Or why. Maybe I was in a car wreck that left me in a coma, and that's why I have an unnerving feeling any time I'm in a car. Perhaps this is a memory from my last moments in the Awake. Or maybe I'm sick and feverish, dragging through an insufferable dream. Maybe I've been out for weeks or months, but I don't think it's so long because I can still hear voices talking to me—Mama, Dad and Violet—all in fervent undertones. I hear them when I'm drifting off to "sleep" at night.

"Wake up, honey," says Mama, brushing the hair from my forehead.

"We're right here," says Dad.

"I love you, Heather. Please come back." Violet breathes these words against my ear, ones we were never brave enough to say when I was awake. I hear them clearly now. So, I probably haven't been sleeping that long. Even the most devoted friends and family members eventually give up. Don't they?

But they're always there, when I'm quiet and still enough, just before I drift off to sleep at night. Yes, I "sleep" here, but it's not real, just a moment of darkness before I'm "awake" again. It's part of the dream.

I've created this world as a dim reflection of the Awake. I know the Awake is better than what I have here, this flurry of days, crammed with school and band and homework. Eating, drinking, and talking inanities with other students. I'm not quite sure where these things begin and end. I'm just piecing together memories as I go along, creating them from my subconscious recollections of the Awake.

In my bedroom here, a crisp poster of Lawrence Olivier hangs above my bed. He was a great actor in the black-and-white days. This poster is a symbol, a reminder of my Dad—my real Dad—not "Father" who exists here, divorced from "Mother," and who has part-time custody of me, but is mostly absent. "Mother" is also on the periphery of my existence. I see her morning and night, bookending my days at Marquette High School. This has *got* to be a dream. I know in the Awake that Mama and Dad are together and happily married, and we have breakfast together at the dining table every morning.

I asked Mother once how she knew she was actually awake.

She rubbed an itch on her nose with her wrist, her hands shiny from preparing raw chicken. "Good question. I think if I were dreaming, I'd be on a beach and not stuffing bread crumbs up a chicken's butt."

Mama would never have answered that way. We'd have sat down together and talked about existentialism and the nature of reality. Instead, I just got out the other board and cut up the vegetables because, even in a dream (even to people who don't exist!), I can be a decent person. That's part of the problem, I guess. I've become too attached.

Dreams aren't easy to escape. It's these emotional ties keeping me here, and my biggest bind is Mark.

Mark is my dream representation of Violet. He used to be faceless, like the rest of the people around me, but he filled in, strong and vivid, as I got to know him better. He's handsome and lean, with a good-natured face and a touch of acne, which teenagers can't seem to help, even in a dream. Probably Violet has pimples too, but they don't matter. If I try hard enough I can remember her short, brown hair curling right over her temples, the funny quirk to her mouth, and her pointed canine teeth that give her a sweet, wildish expression when she smiles.

I don't remember how Mark and I met, which is how dreams go, but somehow he's become the friend who walks with me at school and the person I trust the most—except I haven't been honest enough to tell him about Violet. I once tried the dream question on him, though, posing it casually, like it didn't really matter.

"Do you ever wonder what's a dream and what's real? Like, could we be dreaming right now, only thinking we're awake?

Mark didn't laugh. I knew he wouldn't. He shrugged, then grinned.

"That's too speculative for me. If it's a dream, it's a pretty good one. I hope it comes back tomorrow night." He squeezed my hand in a friendly way. I could have let him continue to hold it, and we would have walked down the street, twined at the fingers, like he wanted.

But I just couldn't do it. Of course, it didn't really hurt his feelings. Dream people don't have feelings.

Later that night though, over burgers, he was unusually broody. He smeared his fries through the last bit of ketchup and chewed for a long time, looking sad. "Do *you* think this might be a dream, then? Us eating dinner here? Do you think *I'm* a dream?" he asked me. There was more in his voice then, something like scorn, and I laughed off the idea as preposterous.

He tried to hold my hand again that night, and I let him.

Mark's persistent for a dream. He's my best friend here. I can't go a day without seeing him, and that's why I'm still sleeping and not with Violet and my real parents. I need to make a break, to destroy the feelings holding me here.

I'm doing it tonight. That's the reason I'm putting on my favorite skirt and top and putting my hair up. Mark invited me on a picnic. "We can drive up the coast road to Maybell. Just you and me."

My outfit and makeup might give Mark the wrong impression, but I'm hoping that preparing myself here will affect my awakening. Maybe my thoughts will be lucid, and my first words will be clear. I'll say, "I love you. I'm so glad you never left me." And everyone at my bedside will be able to hear me despite whatever tubes are up my nose or down my throat. And my face won't be all swollen and distorted. A girl can dream, right?

I know exactly what Mark's planning for tonight—he'll ask me to be his girlfriend, or to "go out" with him. Codifying a relationship in such a specific way seems a little bit silly, but I also find the intentionality to be brave and charming. If he were Violet, I'd fall all over myself. But first I have to get back to her.

Mark knocks, I open, and he smiles a brilliant smile, one brimming with hope and anticipation. There's a funny shyness there, and—I'm projecting, I know—a shadow of hesitancy. I feel it too for a moment, but squash it. I'm going to awaken soon; I'm not going to let anything distract me.

He opens the car door for me, and I'm pleased to spot a wicker picnic basket in the back seat, rather than a cooler. I've always hoped for an old-fashioned romance. I get in the car and put my purse on my lap. It's heavy. I didn't realize how heavy a pistol was, but this one is like an anvil on my thighs. I'd never even seen the gun before, but I took a guess and, sure enough, there was one in the drawer of Mother's bedside table. Just where my subconscious would put one, for a single mother afraid of home invaders.

"Do you want some music?" Mark's hand is shaking just a bit as it hovers near the radio.

"No thanks. Maybe we can just talk."

But we don't. I'm too nervous, as is Mark. Up we go, winding along the coast road, sun like music pouring over us. There is a sheer cliff face below us, overlooking the churning white water of the Pacific. It gives me an ugly feeling and makes my stomach roil. The gun feels heavier on my legs, even though it doesn't really exist. My feet are cold.

"Are you ok?" He chances a glance at me as we swing left, hugging the rocky slope that stretches far above us. I close my eyes and grab the handhold above the door.

"You're just going kind of fast is all," I manage.

"Sorry," he pulls his foot off the accelerator, but not far enough for my liking. His nervousness grows with my own. "I've been really looking forward to tonight." He sucks his bottom lip in between his teeth. "I think you know how I feel about you."

I squirm in my seat, and I can't help but blink toward him. He's quite pale, breathing through slightly parted lips. *Poor guy.* Then I remember, I shouldn't feel bad for him. He doesn't exist. That's why I have the gun.

All I have to do is break our connection.

My fingers twitch on my bag. I remind myself that the trigger is my escape.

"I want, I want you to know. . . " Mark's face goes steely, his eyes fierce. The car engine roars as he slams the accelerator to the floor. The seat kicks me forward and my head slams back into the headrest. I fumble for my gun, but my purse is gone. My fingers clench the stem of a rose. My dream is spiraling away. The thorns bite hard, and my palm goes sticky with blood.

"You're just a dream," Mark says.

His lips pull back in a snarl of determination.

We smash through the guard rail and plunge.

The Problem with Heaven

The boy's black curls dripped steadily as he rubbed the water from his eyes. He wore cut-off shorts revealing scraped knobs of knees, and a red T-shirt pasted to his body with the damp. When his hands dropped he froze, like they all do at first, and he stared time away while his cheeks pinkened and the dusky color faded from his lips. Then, realization struck and the cherubic face shattered into an expression of perfect amazement.

God, I love that. Little kids know where they are immediately—bruised, bald, beaming, it doesn't matter. And kids adjust so quickly, it's like they've always been here. They're so much different than the adults. It always takes a while to convince *them* they've actually arrived.

The boy ran several steps toward me then stopped to look behind him. Lots of kids do that too.

"Is Mama coming?" His lashes were long and damp, giving him a heart-breakingly innocent look. He couldn't have been more than six years old. I couldn't imagine the grief of those he had left behind.

"She is, Aiden. Your mother will be here after a while. You just come with me and I'll get you settled. My name's Aelred."

The boy threw himself at my legs and hugged tightly. "Hey, Aelred."

I laughed and tousled his curls as his dampness seeped through my robe. He would be dry soon enough. The world passes away more quickly than you can imagine.

He slipped his hand into mine, and I led him toward the gates of the Glorious City. Around us, several other arrivals were being embraced by family and friends, or greeted by Citizens like me. Reunions rang with laughter and cries of delight, but no tears. Tears aren't possible here. Pain isn't permitted, and there's no extreme of joy so different from the consistent happiness of our existence that it could possibly evoke tears.

As we walked, I kept an eye out for Aiden's forebears. Typically it's only a matter of minutes before we place people, and eager family members often attend the arrival. But time is an odd thing in eternity. It wasn't necessarily unusual that no one had been present at Aiden's arrival; surely his people were somewhere nearby.

We passed through the gates, and Aiden marveled at the buildings and gardens and parks. Innumerable hues of green, pink, and yellow filled our vision. Songs of birds, voices, falling water layered over one another, the one I liked best naturally growing louder in my ears depending on my mood. Silence when sound was unwanted. Always, only what I wanted. Endless ease and pleasure.

Citizens smiled as we passed by, while Aiden exclaimed at each new delight.

"Oooh, look at the fountain!" he cried. We paused to admire the frosty clear jets of water launching into the sky and falling back into the pool in a diamond spray.

I wondered if he'd be drawn to the even more splendid Crystal Fountain, or if it would hold the same basic attraction as every other feature of the City. You never can tell. I wondered momentarily how Aiden came to be here, if it had to do with that same love of water, but it's not something I ask new arrivals anymore.

So many people have terrible stories. Truly horrifying. And yet, as they calmly recount their final moments in the world, I don't experience the type of grief and revulsion I think should accompany such harrowing accounts. Shouldn't a painful, fearsome death evoke some sort of harmonic anguish in me? It always ends with the new arrival and I just starting helplessly at one another, and I say something like, "Well, that was Before. You'll never have to face anything like that again." And they say, "Yes, that's good. I'm glad."

In the end, all I said to Aiden was, "It *is* a beautiful fountain, isn't it? There are lots of them here. As many as you want." But Aiden didn't want to stop to enjoy the fountain for any longer than it took to skip around it twice it; he just tugged me down the path.

We continued on and on, through the wide cheerful streets filled with people, and the air filled with the scent of Lily of the Valley. Still we found none of Aiden's forebears.

Don't worry," I told him. "There's never anything to worry about here." The words were wasted, though; Aiden wasn't the least bit anxious. He skipped along holding my hand and warbling like a songbird. He was dry now, except for his sneakers, which left damp, shining streaks on the glassy gold street.

Plenty of time, I told myself. Nothing but time here.

I wondered momentarily if he might be some sort of relative of mine, if I might be one of Aiden's great, great, great grand-relations. It had happened before. I had thousands, if not hundreds of thousands of blood relations here, but those ties became less and less meaningful as time went on. Or rather, all ties became equally important. I can't tell the difference.

I smiled down at Aiden, imagining that he was one of mine, and that I could enjoy him in a special way, at least for a while.

I led him out the East Gate toward the orchard and found Samina waiting. She was couched lazily in the shade with her robe pooled around her in radiant white. I leaned back against a welcoming tree and let Aiden dart away to chase a butterfly jangling among the flowers.

"Cute lad," Samina said.

"Painfully cute," I agreed, and we both laughed at my little joke.

That's the problem with Heaven, I guess. No pain. No change. No tears. No night. No stars or sun or moon, for the Light outshines them all. It sounds bizarre, I know. But time changes everything.

And I had loved Orion once, an eternity ago.

A branch leaped from my hand with a leafy rustle as I plucked two apricots. I handed one to Samina.

She examined it impassively before taking a bite. "I didn't care for apricots Before," she said with a sigh. "But I like everything now."

I made a sympathetic sound, sniffed my own sunny apricot, and pressed it to my mouth.

Exquisite.

I ate half and discretely tossed the rest away.

"I've told you that already, haven't I?" Samina brushed off her robe as she rose. "It's so hard to find anything new to say."

She had said that before, too.

"How was your assignment?" I asked, changing the subject. "How'd the old lady take it?"

"Oh, she was surprisingly pleasant."

"Good, good then," I said.

Elderly folks figure out where they are almost as quickly as the kids, but sometimes they're angry. "What the hell took so long?" they want to know. (Of course, they don't actually say that—no one says those sorts of things here—but you can tell they're thinking it.)

Samina rested her chin on my shoulder, and I felt her smile against my neck as we watched the boy caper about. She had been so quiet lately; had we been anywhere else I might have called it unhappiness or restlessness.

"Doesn't he have some place to be?" she finally asked.

"I suppose he must. I can't seem to find it, though."

"Truly?" Two tiny lines I'd never seen before appeared between Samina's dark eyebrows. "I've never heard of that happening."

Now *that* was saying something. I'd worked Arrivals since my cousin, mistaking me for a deer in Kemphall Forest, planted an arrow in my chest; Samina had been here long, long before that.

More lines sketched themselves across her face, and I couldn't help but reach out and touch her. I brushed a finger lightly down the wrinkles between her brows, and they disappeared under my touch. Suddenly, a familiar but fleeting memory stirred inside my head. I seized upon it before it slipped through my conscious like so much dry sand.

A girl. A spray of freckles across a delicate nose. The chimes of her laugher. Her green eyes merry, but suddenly serious as I took her in my arms. Silk-smooth breath against my jaw. Our lips meeting and then—

And then, what? I could never squeeze more from that memory. I had asked other Citizens: some laughed, some seemed nostalgic, still others (like Samina) gave blank, helpless shrugs, but no one could paint the remainder of that scene for me.

Aiden's plaintive voice jolted me from my reverie. I looked down into his upturned face to see his bottom lip quiver.

"I'm *so* sorry," he said again.

He thrust his pudgy hands toward me and, opening them clam-style, revealed a shimmering butterfly, blue wings vibrant as sapphires—immobile in death.

I went ice cold as I tilted his hands back and forth in my own to get a better look. It was impossible.

Samina recoiled, her hand fluttering to her mouth.

"Did *you* do this?" I nearly choked on the words.

Aiden shrunk back, and something strange flickered behind his soft features, but I couldn't name it.

"How?" I demanded.

He cringed and shook his head, and the wings glimmered in his trembling hands. I hadn't seen death in millennia. Not since I'd come here—I hadn't even considered it a possibility. The permanence of everything was too strong. The image of life extinguished was unfathomable. I was almost horrified. Almost angry. Almost frightened.

"Oh, Precious. Don't fret!" Samina gathered her composure as quickly as she had lost it; she swept Aiden into her arms and clasped him to her breast. She stroked his head for long seconds as the boy made juicy snuffles, his hands still sheltering the dead butterfly. I had known Samina for centuries, but had never seen her like this, comforting a child. None had ever needed comfort.

Samina hadn't had the chance to be a mother Before; it seemed a terrible shame.

She cradled Aiden's hand and considered the dead insect they held.

"It's so beautiful," she breathed. "I didn't remember they were so beautiful." I suppressed a shudder and let her shake the butterfly from Aiden's palm into mine.

While I stared helplessly at the weightless blue in my hands, I came to understand what she meant. Heaven was filled with butterflies, but not one had seemed as beautiful to me as this one. The transience of its life added immeasurably to its loveliness.

"Come now. You're coming with me," Samina murmured into Aiden's hair.

We swept away, the three of us, deeper into the orchard, toward Samina's manor.

There were few Citizens in the orchard today, and those who saw us grinned and winked at Aiden in his worldly garb.

"Smile," Samina whispered to him. "We're all happy here."

As we entered the courtyard, Samina raised her lovely face to me, and I knew what she wanted me to do before she asked. I had no idea if it could be done, but I had to try—even if I couldn't hope it was possible. Hope, as the Scriptures say, is fulfilled in Heaven; there is no more need for it.

"You'll take it . . . somewhere?" She nodded toward the secret in my fist.

I nodded, struck mute. This—death—was something that had never happened before in the Kingdom. This was terribly wrong.

Would there be a punishment if the body were to be found?

There hadn't been punishment here since the Beginning.

"I'll hide it," I told her.

Samina's eyes glistened. She reached out to me just like she had embraced Aiden, and I wondered if I was trembling as much as he had. I could see how much this meant to her.

Hope could not exist here.

But love remained.

I sprinted through the orchard and through the fields toward the rocky foothills. Perhaps the butterfly could be hidden in the shale. I simply could not place this corruptible body in holy ground. Perhaps rock wouldn't count.

I ran for a long time, but I never grew weary, and by the time I reached the slopes, the air had filled with gold dust, as near as Heaven ever grows to night. I opened my hand, half-anticipating the tiny flutter of wings that would not come, and found there. . . nothing at all.

I stared in disbelief at the lines that criss-crossed my empty palm. Disbelief gave way to bewilderment. I knew I hadn't dropped it, and yet it was gone. Not even blue dust from the wings remained on my skin.

This was some sort of trick!

Suddenly, I knew what had been hidden behind Aiden's inscrutable look, and my stomach fell.

Deceit.

That boy had meant to kill the butterfly. He had intentionally brought death into the Kingdom. And he had deceived us.

Samina! She was alone with him.

I ran back to the cottage on eagles' wings, faster than I had ever run. I threw open the door and found the room empty, except for Aiden, who sat on a table, his short legs swinging beneath him. He had dropped the affected grief, and met my face with perfect serenity.

"Where is she?" I demanded.

Aiden raised a shoulder. "Samina? I don't know, exactly."

"Your best guess then," I growled, advancing toward him, but Aiden didn't bat an eye at my bravado.

"You don't need to worry about her you know. Samina's very brave. She was ready."

"She doesn't have to be brave," I protested. "There's nothing to fear here!"

"Exactly," said Aiden mildly. "But you have to ask yourself the question: do you believe there's something *more* than here?"

I blinked stupidly. "There's. . . *Before*," I managed, but I knew what Aiden's reply would be even before he opened his mouth.

"Can't there be *After*, too?"

My knees went weak, and I leaned hard into the doorframe.

"What are you? Some sort of teacher? A m-missionary?" I stammered.

"That's one way to put it." The boy grinned, his cheeks plumping like ripe figs. His insouciance was beginning to grate on me, even as I grew oddly . . . fearful?

No, surely not fearful, not here.

"A murderer then?" I countered. "You *killed* that butterfly. You killed something beautiful!"

The boy became suddenly serious. "I'm here to show people a better way."

The little hairs on the back of my neck prickled. I had forgotten that sensation.

"What did you do to Samina? Where is she?"

"She's gone to a better place," Aiden said with only the faintest lightening of his expression.

I had heard that saying before. A cliché. Where had I heard that?

"No! No she's not," I argued. "Where *is*—?"

Aiden held up his hand to stop me then pressed a finger to his lips. His brown eyes were deep and fixed. *Wait.*

Across an unimaginable distance, I could hear it too. The far-off wailing of a newborn babe. The sound was thin and quavering as spider silk and finally faded away into silence.

The words were out of my mouth before I knew I would say them.

"Can I go too?"

Aiden smiled. "If you like."

My legs turned to water then. The floor rushed up at me, and I caught myself hard on my hands and knees. I was panting.

When I raised my head, the boy was kneeling beside me. I saw the kindness on his face and the blue dust glimmering on his fingers as he turned his palm toward me.

I felt a thundering in my chest. How long had it been since I had felt anticipation?

It almost didn't matter what happened next, so long as it was new. Unexpected. Unknown.

Almost.

"Will I see her again? Samina?"

Aiden cocked his head, like a thoughtful bird.

"I don't know. What do you think?"

"I hope I will."

The boy's smile widened. "Then you're half-way there already."

I reached toward him, and all was dust and darkness.

Then, a blinding light.

Fowl Play

This story was inspired by Mike, a Wyandotte rooster who lived for 18 months after being beheaded in the 1940s. Every May, the town of Fruita, Colorado, hosts a two-day festival in his honor.

Tawny's shoulders toasted brown in the afternoon sun, and she could see the skin flaking from her nose. Absently, she scraped dirt from under her fingernails as she strolled past the handful of booths that made up the traveling carnival. It was the high afternoon. The sun baked the ground and created little pools of shimmering heat in the distance. Tawny was among the only carnival-goers at that hour, and even those people working the booths were listless and disinclined to holler up business. Her mother was in bed, as was typical near the end of the month, and Roy was at work, so no one would know if she shirked an hour's labor.

The dusty fairgrounds housed a dozen food vendors and a decrepit Tilt-a-Whirl and merry-go-round; otherwise the carnival consisted mainly of a half-dozen sideshow acts promising unbelievable sights. "The Strongest Man Alive," boasted one. "The World's Smallest Horse," proclaimed another. *Probably a dog,* thought the girl suspiciously, for though she was only nine, Tawny was no fool.

There was one structure, however, set back a bit from the others. A sign out front read "Evening Entertainment Only. For Discriminating Gentlemen." Tawny wasn't quite sure what went on in there.

On the east end of the grounds stood a raised platform covered by a makeshift roof. An unpretentious sign in stenciled, red letters said, "See Mike the headless rooster. 3 cents."

A barrier of hay bales lining the platform hid the presumably hideous Mike from view.

A woman sitting in the shade on one of the bales noticed as Tawny paused to read.

"It's true, girlie. A real-live, headless rooster."

Tawny shaded her face with her hand and squinted at the woman. She was solid and strong, with her hair pulled into a messy bun that gave her a peculiar, uneven look about the face.

"'Real-live headless?" Tawny repeated. "How do you keep him alive?"

The woman grinned, revealing several prominent gaps in her mouth where teeth should have been. "I dribble ground corn and water down his food hole with an eye-dropper."

Tawny's cracked lips pinched in an expression of ancient skepticism.

"Come on in," said the woman.

"Can't. Ain't got three cents."

Now, that wasn't exactly truthful of Tawny. Fact was, Tawny had three whole dimes buried by the elm stump at the front of her family's shack, where Roy, her step-father, wouldn't find them and spend them on drink. But the woman didn't have to know that.

"It's not worth going home for them, anyway," said the old woman, cryptically. "Come on in, girlie, no one else around here today. Come on! I ain't gonna bite you."

Tawny negotiated the weathered boards that made for stairs and slipped into the cool darkness under the roof. It took her eyes a moment to adjust, and she followed the sounds of scratching rooster feet until she spied a fat feathered body and scaly legs, like those of any other rooster, fenced inside the corral of hay bales. Anxious that it might, in fact, be a headless rooster, Tawny steeled herself before allowing her gaze to follow the fat body up to the little stump where the head should have been. The severed neck was dried and healed over, and horny as an old callus. Tawny lowered herself to her knees and craned herself over the enclosure until she spied the strange, brownish hole in the bird's neck.

The woman was making low sounds of admonition in her throat, and Tawny drew back a hairsbreadth.

Mike, despite his obvious handicap, seemed as content as any chicken the girl had ever seen. He strutted in small, aimless circles, fluttering his wings every so often and scratching. Tawny could almost hear his low clucks and roostery growls, except, of course, that he didn't make any.

"He's a quiet pet, but a good 'un."

"Yes, Ma'am. I reckon so." Tawny wondered suddenly if the woman could read her mind.

"Sit down, girlie, before you fall over."

Tawny didn't hesitate. She dropped to her knees, catching herself forearms first on the bale; and a burst of air exploded from her lungs. She had been hoeing all afternoon in the scraggly corn patch, and hauling water to the collards and turnips and all the other root vegetables whose thirst could never be slaked.

Roy had forbidden her mother to work once they had married. No taking in laundry, and certainly not the beautiful sewing that had supported them before he came along. Roy wouldn't have his woman working. No sir! Better to have a little girl scratching in the dirt for something to eat. Yes indeed, that was the way Mr. Roy L. Hamner knew to be right. Roy himself worked in the hen houses for Mr. Camden, when the urge struck him. A thirsty urge, mainly.

Tawny looked away from the rooster, down to where a few bleached threads pulled tight across her knees. She remembered back to the pleated dresses she had worn years ago—before her father had died, and before Roy had come along. Calico or no, Mama's homemade dresses had made Tawny the finest-dressed child in the county.

"Hard work today?"

"Most days," Tawny replied.

At that moment Mike ran into the hay bale beside her. He fell backward, flapped, and scrabbled at the air for a moment. Tawny reached out to set him upright, but the woman called her off.

"He'll be fine. Just fine! Don't you worry about Mike." And sure enough, before she finished speaking, Mike was on his feet again, and going about his blind wanderings.

"H-how did he get. . . like that?" Tawny asked.

The woman gave short cough in the back of her throat.

"My man done it," she said. "I always told Mr. Dean he could have any of the other pullets, but to leave Mike alone. He was my baby.

Had the run of the yard and anything he wanted. One night we argued, Mr. Dean and me. A spit-flyin', bruise-making sort of argument." She cast a shrewd eye at Tawny. "You probably know the kind."

Tawmy gave her a tiny nod. Roy had grabbed her on several occasions, leaving fingerprint-shaped purple and blue marks around her arm. And once a darkened cheek.

"So, Mr. Dean, he storms out," the woman continued, "an' I don't see him for a while, but when I do, it's because I hear Mike flapping and screeching. Then, I seen the glint on the ax blade just before Mr. Dean brings it down." The woman shrugged then, a spastic jerking movement, and spoke no more of the scene. "But later that night, when I go out to see Mike, I find him standing upright, sleeping with his stump under a wing, just like he didn't know any better. Maybe he don't."

Maybe not, except for the running into things, Tawny supposed.

"Yes, he's a happy enough bird, and I'm glad to have him. Makes good company."

"So, you hooked on with the carnival? What about your husband?" Tawny asked.

"Ohhh. He died," said the woman, and the temperature under the ramshackle roof seemed to drop another degree or two. "But Mike, he's no ordinary bird," she continued.

Tawny could see that.

The woman leaned forward, curving her ramrod of a back.

"He grants wishes."

Tawny blinked. It was absurd, but she couldn't help but humor the idea—at least for a moment.

Well then, why haven't you used yours?

The question never reached Tawny's lips, though. Past experience had taught her the benefit of silence. Still, she wondered; Tawny had hundreds of wishes, and if she had a headless rooster that could grant them, she certainly wouldn't be making three cents a peek at it.

"See for yourself. Get down there next to him and whisper your wish at ol' Mike."

Tawny didn't really want to, but then, the woman wasn't really asking.

"Get down there. You wanted to look," the woman insisted. "Get in real close."

Tawny obeyed, as she was taught. She leaned in, lying across the bale, and the straw pierced tiny holes into the soft skin of her belly. Oddly enough, the rooster seemed to sidle a little closer to her.

"Whisper it," prompted the woman. Her eyes were alight with anticipation. "Can't let anyone else know. Not even me."

Tawny swallowed and stared hard at Mike. Of her hundred wishes, only one came to mind as she leaned reluctantly toward the distasteful, headless stump.

"I wish Roy would. . . go away," she said, finally. She didn't dare speak her true wish, not even to a decapitated barnyard bird.

Mike bobbed, as if nodding with his entire body. Suddenly, he stretched his wings and flapped wildly, stirring up dust and tiny slivers of straw. Tawny jerked back on reflex and threw up her arm to shield her face from the bird's thrashing.

From the far corner, Tawny heard the woman's hoarse laughter, and the rooster ran off and plowed into another hay bale. She felt the heat rise in her cheeks. Turning, Tawny saw the woman, bent double, propping herself with an elbow on her knee, and trembling with the strength of her mirth.

So, you didn't get your three cents, Tawny thought, *but you got a laugh.*

"Have a good day, Ma'am," Tawny said, trying to hang on to some dignity as she stepped from the platform. Her eyes were watering from the dust, but she didn't want to wipe them. The woman might have thought she was crying.

The woman gasped mid-laugh. "Yes, girlie. I will."

Back home, Tawny prepared a meager dinner of onions and collards. If Roy would get home they might have some eggs, but dusk had come on and still he hadn't returned. Tawny's mother didn't speak of it of course, and ate the food in her usual silence.

She did not speak at all until sundown when Barnett, a lanky man with a mild expression and drooping moustache, came to the house. He stood in the tremulous light that sifted through the kitchen curtain onto the front porch.

"Is your mother home," he asked Tawny.

"Yessir. "

Barnett tugged his moustache uneasily as her mother made her way to the door. Tawny's mother had pulled her shawl tightly around her shoulders and was gripping it hard in one hand.

Tawny shuffled backward. Out of sight, but not beyond earshot.

"I'm sorry to tell you," the man's voice said. "But Roy's dead, Ma'am."

Clearly, he didn't expect her to faint or cry out. He probably knew too much of Roy's temperament, but his voice was gentle anyway. "Heart attack, we reckon," Barnett explained, "but. . ."

"But?"

There was a pause, and Tawny thought the man might be tugging his moustache again.

"Well, there's probably going to be some talk going around. Some folks saw, and you just can't keep folks from talkin'."

"What is the talk?" her mother said, beginning to sound anxious.

Barnett cleared his throat. "It was kind of odd. See, just before Roy. . . well, some folks say he came screaming out of the hen house, carrying on about how the hens were attacking him, trying to scratch his eyes out."

There was a pause before her mother spoke, but her voice was clear. "Drunk?" she asked.

"Suppose so, Ma'am." Barnett's voice was apologetic.

Tawny sat in a corner chair, draped in shadows as Barnett and her mother made quiet arrangements for Roy's body. Tawny's throat constricted painfully, making it hard to swallow down the fear that, somehow, someone might possibly suspect her hand in this. She also wondered if she shouldn't feel guilty until, alone once more, her mother turned to her with the faintest shadow of a smile.

"I suppose I'll take up the sewing again," she said. "Make you a new dress. Cover those bare shoulders of yours, hm? Time you learned to sew, too."

Tawny's mother rose and placed a kiss on her daughter's dusty head.

Many years later, when Tawny was a wispy-haired grandmother, she sat contentedly in her air-conditioned living room, fondly watching her granddaughters running around in dresses she had made. And she ate well, though her family never served chicken for Sunday dinner, for Tawny would not eat it.

And when the youngest grands asked why Granny didn't like chicken, she'd say,

"Oh, I like chickens fine. That's why I don't eat them—outta respect."

And her grown children would shake their heads, and her grandchildren, giggle.

If you had gone to see "Mike the Headless Wonder Chicken" during his (post-head) life as a sideshow exhibit in 1945/'46, you could have expected to pay up to 25 cents for the privilege. His owners, Clara and Lloyd Olsen, took Mike (and his unattached head) on a U.S. national tour, visiting New York, Los Angeles, Atlantic City, and other major cities. By all accounts, he was a healthy rooster, weighing nearly 8 pounds at the time of his death. (When Mr. Olsen beheaded him, in anticipation of a chicken dinner, Mike had weighed just over 2 ½ pounds.) Unfortunately, death eventually caught up with Mike for good. One night, while returning home from a road trip, Mike began to choke. The Olsens were unable to find the eyedropper they typically used to clear out Mike's esophagus (one may assume the choking was a relatively common occurrence, considering they carried an eyedropper specifically for that purpose), and Mike passed on to that happy, free-range chicken yard in the sky.

For more (yes, there's more!) about Mike and his festival, visit
http://www.miketheheadlesschicken.com

The Cupboard

"Don't open that cupboard," Mrs. Alvarez warned. "The head's in there."

My hand stopped abruptly in mid-air as I noticed a faint red smear on the cupboard door.

Ketchup, I told myself. Or raspberry jam. Nevertheless, a tremor of revulsion jittered down my backbone, and I drew my hand away.

Mrs. Alvarez watched me thoughtfully from the couch where she spent many of her waking hours. Her eyelids gaped murky pink around watery blue eyes, and her skin resembled a dried mushroom, wrinkled and dappled with degrees of aged brown where her arms protruded from her sleeves. She tried to reassure me with a smile.

"It won't hurt you. I don't want you to have to see it is all."

"Oh. Well, thanks," I said. "But . . . can I take it out for you? Throw it away, maybe, so you don't have to worry about it?" If a little play acting could get rid of the imaginary head from the cupboard, it seemed the polite thing to do.

Mrs. Alvarez shook her head slowly. "No, dear. That's nice, but you leave it be. There's an open can of tuna in the fridge. Go ahead and make a sandwich from that; it'll be fine."

She worked the long teaspoon in her glass of weak tea, fished out a chunk of ice, and slurped it into her mouth. I really needed some water, myself. I felt woozy from the heat and thickness of the air; it was too close in the house, and the air was heavy with the stale odor of age. Outside, a steamy heat had made my glasses fog up, and the indoors was sticky-moist despite the diligent whir of the ceiling fan. Mrs. Alvarez's daughter, Connie, had been trying to get the air conditioner repair guys to come for a week, but no one had shown up yet.

I paused before opening the door to the fridge.

"All safe in here?" I asked.

A faint *clink* reached my ears as the ice fell from Mrs. Alvarez's mouth and back into the glass.

"Oh, yes, quite all right."

A breath of cool rushed over me as I opened the door, and I pulled the hair off my neck to take better advantage.

Connie was a retired RN, and she had sold her own home to move in with her mother as Mrs. Alvarez's Alzheimer's progressed. She cared for her mother all day, save a couple afternoons a week when she ran out for groceries and such. On those afternoons, friends from church would come to baby-sit the old woman, and sometimes, on my days off from lifeguarding, I'd put in an hour or two as well.

It made me feel grown-up, but it left me a bit sickish, too. Is this what I could look forward to in my old age? Connie had shared with me some of the odd things Mrs. Alvarez had been seeing recently:

Giant rats gnawing the kitchen stool. Strange men remodeling the bathroom so she was unable to go in and use the toilet. And, most recently, a tiny girl playing in the flower pots outside her picture window. Mrs. Alvarez wouldn't open the window now because the girl might crawl in the house and get lost. According to Connie, Mrs. Alvarez had first "heard" the little girl singing, and then she looked out the window to "see" the nimble creature leaping from one planter to another.

Connie hadn't mentioned a head in the cupboard, though. I'd tell her about it when she got home.

"A little onion and relish in the tuna?" I asked.

"No, no. Just some dill weed and mayonnaise."

I tried not to look at the cupboard as I reached up to the spice rack.

"I hope it's not bothering you." Mrs. Alvarez said. "I just didn't know what else to do. She was there again yesterday, in my lantanas. Such a pretty thing, really. I'm sorry I had to kill her."

My chest tightened. I didn't believe Mrs. Alvarez could kill anything, but the conviction in her voice disturbed me. I felt like I was moving in a weird sci-fi story. Could there possibly exist things she saw that I couldn't? Rats scuttling about the kitchen in some fourth dimension? Dead eyes regarding me from the other side of the cupboard door?

I swallowed and breathed through the discomfort in my ribs. "That sounds horrible," I agreed.

I worked the mayonnaise vigorously into the drained tuna and silently cursed my overactive imagination. Maybe I wouldn't come over here anymore. Mrs. Alvarez never missed my birthday when I was little, but now she rarely remembered my name. It wouldn't be a loss to her. Her weakening faculties hadn't dissuaded me before, but if she was having delusions of killing. . . well, that definitely tested my 'do-gooder nature,' as my brother called it.

Honestly, I was a sucker for public service. It couldn't be considered altruism, I guess, because I got something out of it. The sheer pleasure of helping people. I bought overpriced mints from The Campfire Girls, and participated in litter clean-ups at the local park. I'd even befriended a local stray—a mangy orange cat, half-starved and suspicious, who fattened up on the cat food I left under our carport. These days Garfield bounded across the yard to greet me and meowed belligerently for my attention.

Maybe it was time for Connie to find a new place for her mother to live. It was hard on her; Connie wasn't a spring chicken herself, and full-time caretaking was clearly wearing her down. If Mrs. Alvarez got into a home then Connie could get a break, and I wouldn't have to come over anymore. I was ashamed at the selfishness of the thought, but couldn't deny it either.

I placed the plate on the TV tray by Mrs. Alvarez. Light filtered in from the blinds behind her, illuminating the tiny dust motes like a hazy aureole around her shriveled form.

"I regret having to kill her," she said again. "I thought the plumbers in the bathroom might scare her off, but they didn't. She was pulling off the lantana blossoms though, so I had to do something." As she reached for her food, I couldn't take my eyes from the woman's blue-veined hands, the horny, jaundiced nails and papery skin.

"It wasn't as hard to kill her as I thought," she mumbled. The masticated sandwich made a warm, gluey sound that caused my stomach to pitch. I reached to adjust the fan, but it brought no relief. "I saw you looking at my hands; they're still pretty strong. I can cut chicken off the bone, and I can use a can opener too, so it wasn't very hard. There was more hair than I thought. And more blood. But I got most of it cleaned up."

Sweat streaked down my temple.

"I lured her to me. She thought I was playing, but I most certainly was not," Mrs. Alvarez assured me, as if I had voiced doubt. "And I killed her quick so she couldn't make too much noise."

Her voice droned on as waves of heat and acrid odor lapped over me, and I forced myself to stop listening. I didn't even realize she had stopped speaking until her head lolled to the side, asleep. As if hypnotized, I stood and readjusted her on the couch. She was absurdly light, like stalks of withered day lilies at the end of the season. I positioned her head carefully on a pillow then gathered up her plate and cup and went back into the kitchen.

As I did, something seemed to watch me from inside the cupboard; it called to me with the faint scratching of fingernails on dry skin. The presence there was as real as the warmth of the room, the tinge of putrescence filling my nose. It called me forward and, from a distance, I watched my fingers close around the cupboard's door pull. Suddenly, a shadow collapsed in from the edges of my vision. A silent vacuum sucked my eyes into my skull and blackness engulfed me with a roar.

I awoke with the cool tingle from the kitchen tiles on my skin. A flood of fresh air from the open front door flowed over my face, reviving me. I tried to push myself upright as Connie steadied me with her sure, capable hands at my elbow.

"Don't get up too fast, now! Easy. You just sit right there for a moment." She gave me a quick triage, even as I assured her of my soundness.

"My soul and body, but it's a furnace in here," Connie proclaimed, opening a kitchen window. "No wonder you fainted. Thank heavens it's cooling off some outside." A pleasant breeze swept in, whisking away the anxiety and paranoia brought on by the stifling mugginess. Mrs. Alvarez slept peacefully on the couch. The cupboard above appeared perfectly innocent. Clearly, the stain was dried ketchup. How could I have taken it for anything else?

After a glass of cold water, I helped Connie put some groceries away in the fridge just to prove my mettle.

"Now, that's enough. You've done so much already," she said, taking a box of pasta from my hand. "Let me see you home."

"No, please. I'm fine," I protested. Mercifully, Connie did not insist, but made do with thanking me profusely as I headed out alone.

Walking out the door was like emerging from a tomb into a botanical garden. The sun shone brightly, and in spite of the muggy heat, I felt light—newly emancipated. Connie had done her best to keep up the yard for her mother, and the colors awakened my eyes after the dreary darkness of Mrs. Alvarez's home. The azaleas were radiant, and the butterfly bush was filling out in a mass of blossoms.

I could have sung, but I purred loudly for Garfield instead. As I descended the porch, a sunny, yellow and purple cluster of lantana blossoms caught my eye. It lay decapitated beside the planters, next to writhing pools of ants clustered around. . . what? A dead bug? No, on closer inspection, it appeared to be a bit of tuna. Then, I noticed maroon splotches on the planter and the sidewalk. Tiny pinpricks and fat dried gouts of viscous red had attracted their own hosts of tiny harvesters.

The tang of horror, like chewing aluminum foil, filled my mouth, and the screen door clattered open. I looked back in time to watch Connie stumble over the threshold. She clutched the doorframe, her face a tight mask, lips pulled back from her teeth in a silent shriek of terror.

My hand, as if it no longer attached to me, reached out and plucked a tuft of blood-stained cat hair from the blooming lantana.

And I knew Connie had opened the cupboard.

10 Secrets

(of your stuffed animals)

1. You drool when you sleep. Seriously, you're just gushing. Can't you do something about that?

2. On the flip-side, it's not always your fault the bed is wet.

3. Yeah, we know how to work the alarm clock.

4. We control access for the bedbugs, too, so you'd better stop kicking us off.

5. And that dream you keep having about a lion chewing your arm? You might want to have a little talk with Stuffed Simba about that.

6. And speaking of talks, *we're* the ones who found your candy stash. You owe your little brother an apology.

7. We also think you need to do something with Bear-Bear. Sure, you've had him since you were in a crib, but the poor guy is mostly dust mites inside now. If only you could hear them like we do.

8. Remember Sweet Ducky? Yellow and soft, just right for kisses and rubbing against your cheek. "So tiny and sweeeeeet!" Remember how you could cup him in just one hand, and he would peer up at you with his dark, plaintive eyes? Like he was trying so hard to tell you something? Remember how Sweet Ducky disappeared?

   He was a weakling.

9. Anyway, who is that person who appears under your bed at night once you turn out the lights?

10. Yes, we *are* watching you sleep.

(11. The dolls are plotting against you.)

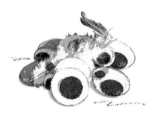

Bugaboo

Melody had the wide, round eyes of a frightened rabbit. She stared at me anxiously from the top of the staircase as I tried to get my bearings; her mother hadn't even introduced us before sweeping out the door.

I reached a hand toward her, in the most harmless way I could manage. "Come on down, I won't bite," I said.

The girl's mouth lifted in a shy smile, and she started down the stairs with a slow, delicate gait. It struck me funny. Most six-year-olds would thunder down like a buffalo or slide down that long, smooth banister.

Maybe she hasn't had a boy babysitter before, I reminded myself.

That was the first thing some kids remarked on when they met me. I never got a ton of jobs; I knew most parents of little girls had a list of girl babysitters to go through, and by the time they got down to me they felt they were scraping the bottom of the barrel. Boy babysitters are suspect.

"I'm Stephan." I knelt to meet her at eye-level.

The smile widened, but still Melody didn't speak.

"So, you'll have to tell me what you want to do tonight," I said. "I'm new here, but you know all the good stuff." Sometimes kids like to take the lead. It makes them feel good to think they're the experts on something. Melody seemed no different in that respect, at least; she grabbed my hand and hauled me into the living room. There didn't appear to be much to do there, so I flopped into a recliner and asked, "Do you have some toys or games you want to play?"

Melody's face drained of color, and her staring eyes widened at me. "Ohh, please don't bounce on the furniture. The Bugaboo doesn't like that."

"The what?" I assumed she was making some sort of joke, but Melody's pinched little features were solemn as a tombstone.

"The *Bugaboo*," she whispered. Melody reached for my hand again, and I thought it was innocent friendliness until I felt the tremor in her cold fingers "The Bugaboo lives in the walls," she said, sidling closer. "And if you make too much noise, he'll come out."

I snapped my mouth shut so hard my teeth clacked. My older brother had scared me with similar tales as a kid, and Melody was taken in as thoroughly as I had been.

"Don't you believe it for a minute," I said. "Someone's just trying to scare you."

The soft, rabbit-eyes took on a hopeful, pleading droop.

"Who told you about the Bugaboo?" I asked, trying to keep my voice calm. I had to resort to lip-reading to understand her silent response.

"Mama."

The answer struck me dumb. Melody's mother was no more than a series of first impressions to me. A severe hairstyle pulled up at the corners of her face. Dramatic walnut-colored eyes. A double-looped strand of multi-colored stones around a long marble neck.

Mrs. Chambers had hired me on a last-minute recommendation (a friend-of-a-friend-of-a-friend) and took no interest in the teenaged stranger with whom she'd be leaving her only child. She'd scarcely looked at me as she shrugged into a full-length raincoat.

"I'll be gone until after midnight. Melody needs to be in bed by nine. No T.V. My cell number's on the fridge," she said. And with that, Mrs. Chambers was gone.

The woman was cold, no doubt about it. If I were being charitable, I might have said that she was just preoccupied tonight, that everyone was entitled to their bad moments, and she'd given me an unfortunate first impression.

But seeing the abject terror Mrs. Chambers had inflicted on her daughter, I wasn't at all inclined toward charity.

A sudden blast of thunder rocketed Melody up onto my lap where she seemed to put out roots—she had no intention of budging. Fortunately there were a few books arranged tidily in the basket next to the chair, and I plucked one at random and asked if she'd like to hear it.

"That's fine," she said. It wasn't enthusiasm, but at least it was something.

I don't think she really listened, but I read to her about garden fairies, lost puppies, and friendly frogs until we'd worked our way through every book in reach.

"Do you want me to get some more?"

Melody shook her head against my chest. She seemed perfectly content to sit there all night, letting me stroke her hair while my legs went numb.

As we rocked, Melody found her voice. She listed for me all the things the Bugaboo didn't like—loud laughter, skipping in the hall, eating anywhere but in the dining room. So many things would raise the Bugaboo's ire.

"What does the Bugaboo do when he comes out of the walls?" I asked.

"He *punishes* you," Melody whispered, and her dark eyes darted around to all corners of the room.

"Well, I'm sure your Mama's just teasing you," I said, though a crueler joke I couldn't imagine. "Have you actually seen the Bugaboo?"

"No, but Mama has."

That surprised me. Most kids I knew would probably say they had at least glimpsed the monster, even if it was only in their imaginations. But not Melody. Probably the Bugaboo didn't like lying.

"Mama talks to him at night and tells him if I've been behaving at school and acting appropriately," she explained.

"I'm sure you're a very good girl," I told her. "I don't think you ever have anything to worry about." I fought down the anger in my voice. Melody's weren't a child's words; they were parroted by a little girl who had heard them too often.

If ever there was a Bugaboo, Mrs. Chambers was it.

A roll of thunder crashed over the house, and Melody started again, cracking her skull against my jaw.

"I don't like thunder," she said.

"I noticed."

Eventually the storm faded and I told her I'd make us some microwave popcorn—to eat in the dining room, of course. Melody waited patiently at a small side table, silently admiring a single orchid in an expensive-looking blue and white pot, while I watched the bag expand in the microwave. The bag was nearly finished when three things happened simultaneously. There was a clap of thunder, a squawk of surprise, and the ominous shattering of some fragile object. I whirled to see Melody cringing in a spray of dirt and porcelain. The orchid lay naked on the floor at her feet.

Melody hunched like a rabbit caught in the flight-or-fight moment just before the fox pounces and snaps her neck. Her eyes were wide and unseeing as her head whipped left and right, trying to anticipate the arrival of the Bugaboo.

Her mouth was moving, but I couldn't hear what she was saying until I was close enough to scoop her up in my arms.

"I didn't mean to. I didn't mean it." Melody was breathless with terror. "I'm sorry. I'm sorry."

I sidestepped the mess, wary of treading in the dangerous-looking shards. "There is no reason to be afraid," I said to her. "I promise. There is no Bugaboo." It became a mantra over the next hour, though I had no idea if she could even understand me, for she never so much as twitched as I held her on the chair.

"There is no Bugaboo." *Except for your mother.*

Melody had no more interest in popcorn and wouldn't let me put her down for an instant. I rocked her in the recliner until she fell asleep from exhausted terror. I carried her upstairs, dressed her in her nightgown, and tucked her safely away in her regulation-made bed. And, I couldn't help it; I placed a little kiss just above one of her fine, soft eyebrows.

"Don't be afraid," I whispered to her. "Sleep well."

Back downstairs, I hurriedly collected the pieces of porcelain pot, swept thoroughly, and wrapped the orchid's roots in a damp paper towel. Though the clock was barely ticking its way to nine, I wanted to get the job done quickly, in case Mrs. Chambers returned early. I even crushed the popcorn bag and stuffed it into the very bottom of the trash can. My stomach was in knots—I couldn't eat a bite, but I felt certain Mrs. Chambers wouldn't like to see the waste.

After that, the night dragged along, and neither book nor television could ease the prickling that ran the length of my spine. I prayed that when Mrs. Chambers said, 'no T.V.' she had meant it only for Melody. But I eventually gave it up; the noise irritated me. Generally a radio or T.V. makes for good company, but in a house haunted by a Bugaboo, it distracts one from hearing its approach.

Stupid, I told myself. *You know there's no such thing as a Bugaboo.* Unfortunately reason and feeling don't always keep company.

There was no restful spot in the house, and I held my breath, creeping between rooms. I eventually settled in the front parlor, a small sitting area that overlooked the leafy drive. I sank into an uncomfortable chair that gave me a full view of the room. Unfortunately, this left my back to the wall. And that's where the Bugaboo lived.

Bugaboo.

Bugaboo.

Something was crawling in the walls. Behind the high crown molding, the upper-end décor, the artwork.

It's Mrs. Chambers—it came from her, I told myself. She *is the Bugaboo.*

Something bad was crawling around inside of Mrs. Chambers. Behind the marble face, the velvet voice, the opaque eyes.

It's her.

Yet the reach of the Bugaboo went everywhere.

I wanted to go upstairs to be with Melody, just for the presence of another human being, but I couldn't move. My eyes glazed. I was hyper-aware of the sound of my breath grating in and out. I just had to survive my own fear, and the watchful approach—return?—of the Bugaboo.

My heart all but stopped when the front door swung open. Had it been anyone else, I would have been glad to see another person in that house, but Mrs. Chambers didn't even greet me. She swept past the room and toward the kitchen, where her raincoat swished as she dropped it on a bar stool. I hurried in after her. "What happened here?" The tendons in her neck stood out against the ropes of her necklace as she stared at the bare table.

"It was an a-accident." I couldn't choke back the stutter. "Melody, uh, I—"

Mrs. Chambers cut me off. "Melody knocked it over?"

"No, it was me, I accidentally—"

"Don't lie to me!" Her voice was an icy hiss. "I'll know if you're lying."

I blinked away, unable to hold her eyes.

"The thunder startled her. It was an accident," I explained. "She didn't mean to do it. She was so scared. And this Bugaboo—!"

A muscle was twitching beside Mrs. Chambers's mouth. "I've told her over and *over* again to keep away from that table!" she snarled, snatching several crisp bills from her clutch. "Thank you for watching her."

She thrust the money at me, and I hesitated. I couldn't let this woman continue to terrorize her daughter.

51

"I was glad to watch her, Mrs. Chambers," I said. "She's a very good girl. Really sweet. *Really*."

"You don't *know*. You have *no* idea." Whatever anger had seized her a moment before drained away before my eyes. Her voice and face were dead, and still something menacing simmered behind that rigid mask. "Take the money and *get out*."

I had no more chance of getting through to this woman than I had of soothing Melody's terror. I would have to find someone else to help me save Melody from this Bugaboo woman. If it could be done at all.

I slipped the money into my coat pocket as she herded me onto the porch. The door shut firmly behind me, like the definitive closing of a coffin lid.

Driving away into the cool, drizzling night, I hated myself for my cowardice. This woman had no qualms about terrifying her daughter with monsters. What would it take to provoke her to violence? Reflecting back on her ferocious expression at the empty table top, and I thought I knew.

Mrs. Chambers wouldn't be able to fight off whatever violence clawed at her. Not for long.

Light shone from the front door's faceted window, tiny specks of illumination like the eyes of a spider, as I pulled back into the drive. I pushed the car door open just in time to hear a blood-curdling shriek from the house. It was followed by a hollow rumble like the evening's now-distant thunder.

I ran up the porch steps and threw open the door. At the foot of the stairs, Mrs. Chambers lay sprawled, gaping on the shining hardwood floor. Her unseeing eyes were fixed on the ceiling, and a long string of polished stones lay in her clawed fingers.

I was frozen in shock until there came a tiny, pained sound from above me. I raised my eyes.

At the top of the stairs, exactly where I had first seen her, stood Melody, her hands pressed to her face, dark eyes peeking above stubby fingers. Long red stripes rose on her legs where the nightgown didn't quite reach. I skirted her mother's body and took the stairs three at a time to reach her.

I gathered Melody into my arms, shielded her from her mother's lifeless body and tucked her face into my neck.

"M-Mama was chasing me," she whimpered. "She hit me with her necklace."

"It's okay. She won't hit you now," I murmured, stroking her head.

"I ran out of my b-bedroom to get away. I was running to the bathroom. I looked back. . ." Melody shuddered against me.

"Did you see your Mama fall?" I managed.

"She didn't fall." Melody's voice was a tiny sigh pressed to my neck. "The Bugaboo pushed her."

A blast of rain blew in from the open door, and the drops shone like tiny beads of amber on the floor.

There's no such thing as a Bugaboo, I wanted to tell her, but the words died in my throat. I called 911 on my cell, and cradled Melody against me in the security of my own car until the police arrived.

Just in case I was wrong.

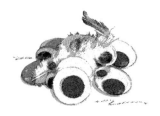

Resurrection

We have erected a monument to commemorate the funeral of a species. It symbolizes our sorrow. We grieve because no living man will see again the onrushing phalanx of victorious birds, sweeping a path for spring across the March skies, chasing the defeated winter from all the woods and prairies of Wisconsin.

Men still live who, in their youth, remember pigeons. Trees still live who, in their youth, were shaken by a living wind. But a decade hence only the oldest oaks will remember, and at long last only the hills will know.

Aldo Leopold, from "On a Monument to a Pigeon," in A Sand County Almanac

Alice bit back a cry of delight. It was almost painful to see the beautiful creatures and not be able to touch them. She glanced up at Dr. Morales, who caught her expression and smiled down at her, eyes glassy. Alice's heart squeezed hard as the bravest little fox poked his nose out of the den and toppled into the open. He was fuzzy, a cloudy tan and gray, with small, tent-like ears and all the swaggering confidence of a nineteen-day old swift fox kit.

"Atta boy, Sinbad," Alice whispered. The male kit was officially K3 in reports, but Dr. Morales had given her—Via-lab's first student intern—the right to informally name the last kit, and "Sinbad" had sprung to mind immediately. K1 had been dubbed Clytemnestra by a pretentious level 1 embryologist and K2 was Remel, thanks to her supervisor. Alice had seen each kit as an embryo before their implantation into their vixen, the red fox (RV1) who had been engineered to carry the foreign embryos. Alice had even watched their births on camera. The first swift foxes the earth had seen in fifty years. They had been snuffed out of existence and then brought back, their very being snatched out of the abyss and revealed again in toddling bodies of fluffy fur, shining eyes and wet noses.

"Do you know, I remember when the resurrected leatherback turtles hatched." Alice's reverence damped her voice; there was no need for her to actually whisper. The foxes' enclosure was soundproofed, so they would only ever hear the "natural" noises piped into their environment.

"You remember the turtles, do you?" said Dr. Morales, surprised.

"I was only three, but I remember."

Since then, she had watched the rebirth of the lowland gorilla and the passenger pigeon and nearly a dozen other species, once extinct.

"Then why don't you do the honor of holo-Feeding this out on the Via-lab band?" said Dr. Morales, and Alice did. She took a few seconds of feed which uploaded automatically to the Infomonde. She worried her trembling hand would distort the holographic image, but it must not have been too badly blurred because in a matter of seconds, several "attas!" popped up in the reply Feed. Icons of smiling faces, applauding hands, and sparkles of confetti holoformed above her screen, one image dissolving as another took its place. She clicked her Feed off after a moment and turned her attention back to the kits, who had all emerged now into the manufactured light and padded curiously through the grass.

It was a relief to know that their entire lives would be protected and monitored here in this custom-tailored fox habitat. All over the world, humans were manucreating animal environments. It was the lack of habitat that had driven some to extinction, like the polar bear; or the fear and hunger of humans that had done in others like the Great White shark and the Albacore Tuna. But now, they had custom environments, like this one. It wasn't perfect, but it was enough for the kits who rolled over one another in play and sniffed the reclaimed air.

Alice didn't realize she was holding her own breath until stars prickled her vision, and she inhaled quickly.

"It's just like a miracle," she said.

"It is. It is a miracle." Dr. Morales shook his head with the beauty of it, but when he turned to face her, he was somber. "And don't let anyone tell you otherwise."

It hadn't been his intention, but those few words struck her like pebbles against a window pane. Cracks spider-webbed through her delight in all directions, and Alice began steeling herself for what awaited her outside.

* * * * *

Alice didn't shield her face as she stepped out of the building. She wasn't a criminal; she didn't need to be ashamed.

Protesters are merely noise, she told herself, and she tried to let their words brush over her like a warm wind.

Fourteen years ago, as Alice watched the leatherback turtles hatch back into the world, she could never have imagined people reacting this way to today's resurrections. There used to be world-wide celebrations every time an animal was resurrected, but now there was little fanfare beyond the Infomonde Feed reaction.

Today, most of the people who showed up at Via-lab were protestors. And if it weren't for the approaching migration of the passenger pigeon, and the demonstrations spread out along their flight path, there might have been more of them.

Right now, there were only a couple dozen protestors or so. People of all colors and ages. She tried to ignore them, but her eyes betrayed her and flickered over a few of the signs. "God created the creatures and called them good." "It is required for all to die ONCE!" And most bewilderingly "The spirit of a man goes upward, and the spirit of a beast goes down into the earth."

Alice had tried to understand, on several occasions, the reason for their anger. She had gone to the websites and watched the interviews. Most seemed to agree that the animals had gone extinct as part of a cosmic plan. That their deaths were ordained and part of an earthly punishment—against humans or against the animals themselves, there seemed to be no consensus. But all seemed to agree that bringing the animals back was equally as wicked as their original annihilation. Alice could only sigh at this, and she flinched as a man began pounding the end of his sign on the ground.

"No playing God!" he bellowed, "No playing God!" The crowd enthusiastically took up the chant around him.

Alice ducked her way through the lot, and hurried toward the bus stop, hoping no one would follow her. It was a wasted worry. She got to the shelter in time to see the bus just a few blocks down. No one looked up from their Feed at her arrival, but Alice felt eyes on her just the same, and her gaze jerked, instinctively, to the watcher across the street.

The girl was still as an anvil. She had dark, penetrating eyes and black hair with hints of copper that caught the sun. Alice blinked, momentarily taken in by the girl's dramatic looks, but then her attention was caught by the simple sign she held in front of her chest.

"Resurrection Is Cruelty" it read.

And then the bus's arrival blocked her from view.

* * * * *

It was just after nine o'clock, and the rain was coming down now in earnest. Alice's parents called to tell her they'd be in late from the fundraiser, and so she took her bowl of ice cream into the den for a solo movie on the couch.

She turned on the light and started so hard the spoon fell out of the bowl.

"What are you doing here?" she yelped, heart pounding.

The girl from the bus stop stood in the middle of the room, tapping furiously at an ancient Feed. "Sorry. I knocked, but you didn't answer." Her hoodie was damp from the rain and her hair was frizzy from removing her hood.

"How did you find my house?" Alice demanded.

The girl never looked up but shook the Feed and scowled. "Look, I'm sorry to just barge in. My name is Noura, and I really want to show you something. I saw you today and thought maybe you were young enough."

"Young enough to what?"

"To be hopeful." She grimaced and banged the Feed with the heel of her hand. In spite of the fact Alice was still trembling from the shock, and her home had been invaded, she felt almost embarrassed for the girl.

"Look, I'm being pretty patient here considering you've just broken into my house," she said. "Say what you want to, then leave." She retrieved the spoon and set the ice cream aside on the lamp table, before putting fists to her hips.

"Ok, ok. I will," Noura muttered. She tapped her Feed several more times and gave a hiss of relief. "There it is," she said. A flick of her wrist and a holograph materialized above the screen—the tender image of a gorilla resting languidly on her side, nursing her droopy-eyed infant.

Alice's suspicion slackened somewhat. She leaned in to see the holograph more closely and smiled. "I've never seen this particular picture before, but that's Soleil and Nassir," she said. "They live in an environment in Congo."

"Wrong. This is Kibwe—that's Swahili for 'blessed'—and her son Mosi, which means 'first child'. Pretty, huh?" There was a cutting bitterness in Noura's voice now. "The day after this picture was taken, Kibwe strangled her baby, and then she hanged herself in her play net. Why do you think she did that?"

Alice scarcely understood the rush of words. She shook her head while sounds of confusion burbled from her mouth.

"Are you sure?" she finally said, following quickly with, "Where did you learn that?"

Noura ignored the questions and tilted her hand until the image flipped. The gorilla mother's face was grim now; one leathery hand pressed her son to her breast while the other squeezed his slender neck. The infant's eyes bulged, and his tongue protruded from his gaping mouth, black and grey.

Alice threw up her hands and turned away. "Why are you showing me this? Where did you even get this?"

"Why do you think no one's heard of it?" Noura replied.

Alice's ire had been refueled by the ugly shock of the photo. "I don't know you from anyone," she snarled. "There are a dozen ways you might have got this image on your phone. It might not even be real."

"It's real." Noura shoved the picture in front of her face again, too close for Alice to even focus on it, and Alice swiped her hand away with a smack.

"So, let's say, for the sake of argument, it's true. That's one tragic, *terrible* event. It's no reason to stop resurrections. That's what you want, isn't it?"

Noura didn't respond, she just stood there, holding a new image between them. This time it was a holofilm. Kibwe was patting her lifeless baby, head back, eyes closed as if grieving, as she leaned against her hammock net. Her free hand idly fingered the rough rope.

"That's terrible," Alice said with a rasp. "Turn it off."

Noura slid the Feed into her pocket. "What's terrible," she said, "is that we bring them back into a world that refuses to make room for them."

"We *do* make room for them," Alice yelped. "We create enormous habitats. Developed just for them. Wh-Why, just today," she sputtered, "we released resurrected foxes into a room—"

"A room!" Noura seemed to crackle. "Like a zoo!"

"Better than a zoo!" Alice argued.

"'We like animals. Yes, we do. Living knick-knacks, in a zoo,'" Noura intoned nastily. "But what's in it for the animals?"

"What kind of question is that? They exist! Isn't that enough? And we do release some animals into the wild. All the ones we can." Alice was practically panting. "You'll see tomorrow. When the passenger pigeon migration passes over."

The migration was already in its fourth day. The living birds were gamely following the manufactured drone birds who would teach them the southward path. There looked to be no reason the migration wouldn't be a complete success, yet Noura's expression was grim.

"Ah, yes. The pigeons."

"It's amazing how well they've done," Alice continued eagerly. "Eight years and the flock has topped 4,000 birds!" It made her a little dizzy just thinking about it. She couldn't understand how Noura stood, brooding and chewing her bottom lip.

"It can't work," Noura said with a sniff. "Their flyways are gone. There used to be hundreds of thousands of those birds. Millions of them. Their flocks would darken the skies for days during the migration. There's really nothing left for them now."

"Where have you been?" demanded Alice. "We've been at this for years! We've planted new flyways. Rooftop gardens. Enormous roosts acres wide. We've repurposed abandoned neighborhoods and entire subdivisions to create the new flyway! It cost more than the actual resurrection did."

Noura's mouth was a bitter line. "You know how they died right, the passenger pigeons?" Alice did, of course, but Noura didn't wait for an answer. "First we deforested the continent, so the pigeons didn't have enough food or shelter. They died by the tens of thousands. In the 1800s, we commercialized their meat for slaves and the poor. They died by the millions. The last one died in a zoo in 1914."

"Her name was Martha," Alice added. She made it a point to always remember names.

Noura shook her head, and Alice reached out and put a hand on her shoulder, half expecting her to jerk away. But Noura didn't move a hair.

"It's terrible what we did. Awful." Alice admitted. "But we know better now. The birds are starting the migration. Everything's in place. Four thousand birds!" Alice was awed by the very idea, but Noura seemed unable to even acknowledge it.

"Four thousand birds isn't enough." She shrugged her shoulder and Alice's hand fell away. "They're colonial animals. It takes thousands upon thousands to maintain the flock. When the original pigeon numbers dropped into the low thousands, they stopped breeding entirely. It's just not enough." She leaned against the dining table now, as if the discussion were taxing. "But it's already too many."

"We don't know that," Alice argued, lumping herself in with the scientists. She hoped that didn't make her sound arrogant. "Everything looks good so far with the birds. And maybe this flock can manage. Maybe it was some other variable altogether that caused the original breeding crash."

"And if not? And they go extinct again?"

"I'm sure that's not going to hap—" Alice began, but Noura wasn't hearing her, and butted in with eerie, false cheer.

"I guess we'll just make some more. We'll just whip up a new batch to ease our collective conscience. We'll say, 'I'm sorry I ran over your puppy, little girl. Let's go to the pound and get another."

"It's not the same," Alice said, growing angry again.

"It's cruel, what you're doing," Noura concluded. "It's flat cruelty. By all means, let's bring them back. But not for our sake—for theirs, and *only* when they can live as they were meant. If we can't do that— if we can't provide them with whole lives—we aren't bringing them back to life at all." Noura pulled her hood over her head, looking out the window now rather than at Alice. The rain was a light shower misting the outside world. "How many times do you think people would have to see an image like that—like Kibwe and Mosi—" she said, "before they could be convinced this is wrong?"

Alice didn't have anything to say to that. One image. One gorilla and baby. It was very sad, but the successes would outweigh the defeats. *They had to,* Alice decided.

"Did you see my Feed today?" she said. "The new foxes came out of their den for the first time this afternoon."

Noura sighed. She drew the hood strings tightly around her face, leaving just a weary expression showing, and stepped out into the softly pattering night.

* * * * *

Alice slept fitfully, eager to see the kits again. She rubbed weariness from her eyes as they mounted the stairs to the observation deck. Overhead were dozens of holoFeeds thanks to the tiny camera eyes hidden throughout the enclosure. The foxes would never be out of sight, whether in their den, hiding in the small thicket, or exploring the hollow log that lay near the "creek" which was piped in from the northwest corner of the room and out the south wall.

But Alice didn't need the holoFeeds today. She peered directly through the one-way glass to see Sinbad and Clytemnestra trotting along the woodpile that partially lined the east wall of the enclosure. She was amazed at how far they had traveled from their burrow. They were in no danger as they had no natural predators, but it seemed unusual, nevertheless. The attentive vixen trotted over and hauled Sinbad back to the den by the scruff of his neck.

"Good Mama," Alice breathed, but no sooner had the vixen turned back to fetch her female kit, than Sinbad staggered out from the mouth of the den, stumbled in weariness down the shallow embankment, and toddled again toward the hidden wall of his enclosure.

Gooseflesh broke out on Alice's neck and back, and she shrugged against a strange oppressive feeling. There was a sound behind her, and she spun, nerves prickling. Dr. Morales was standing in the back corner; he had removed his glasses and was rubbing the bridge of his nose with a knuckle. "Why are they doing that?" she asked him. "They're just hugging the walls. Even though they don't know they're there. . . Do they?" Alice added, suddenly unsure.

Dr. Morales clicked his tongue and frowned ruefully into the enclosure. "It's sometimes one of the side effects. K1 and K3 started up late afternoon yesterday. They rested some during the night, but as soon as we initialized the daylight sequence, they were at it again. Trotting along the perimeter of the enclosure"

"When will they stop? It can't be good for them," Alice said.

The scientist sighed. "Hard to say. Things like this can last an hour or two. Or a day. We'll keep an eye on them, and if they're like this at the end of tomorrow, we'll have to. . . make other arrangements."

A rock landed in Alice's stomach. She heard a voice similar to hers, but surely *not* hers, ask.

"What arrangements?"

Dr. Morales gave her a sad look. "You know we can't keep them in confinement," he said. "You can imagine what it does to them."

Alice shook her head. "But there will only be one kit—just K2 left."

"It's hard. It's a tragedy whenever something like this happens, but we can always start over. We can tweak the genetics next time, make the next foxes more suitable for their lives in the enclosure." Dr. Morales raised an eyebrow at her. "That's part of the miracle, isn't it?"

Alice squirmed. "But if we could provide them bigger habitats, or. . . if we could convince people we need to restore the lands? Provide them with their original lives? We've done a little of it already—for the pigeons."

"But at what expense?" The automatic response was evidence the scientist had considered these questions before. "Think of the billions of dollars these projects have already cost and how hard it was to restore what few land resources we *do* have. You've got to convince people it's worth it."

"Can't we?"

Dr. Morales laughed then, a bitter sound. "Look around. Think back, Alice. Have we ever seen anything like that? Human nature doesn't change fast enough. If something is not in our immediate interest, we ignore it. Or we convince ourselves it isn't important at all. We do what we do, and whoever survives, survives. That's just a simple fact. I don't know what it would take to change human nature."

"Maybe it *could* change." Alice was practically shouting now. "If people could be made to understand."

Dr. Morales gave her the ghost of a smile. "I wish I had your optimism again. Optimism is for young people."

Alice dimly recalled Noura's words from the previous night. "Maybe you're young enough. You might be able to hear."

She turned and gripped the window sill hard, unable to tell whether she wanted to cry or throw up. Every system in her body seemed tangled. "Maybe someone should just tweak *our* genetics," she muttered.

The scientist patted her avuncularly on the shoulder, and it was all Alice could do to not snap at his hand like a wild dog.

* * * * *

For the rest of the day, Alice noted the actions of the foxes in her digital journal.

The vixen spent the day alternately hunting the small mammals that also lived in the habitat and returning to the burrow to check on K2, who showed less inclination to explore than her littermates. She apparently gave up on Sinbad and Clytemnestra.

Rather, it was Alice who was preoccupied with the doomed kits. Alice stared, heart in her throat as they gamely staggered along the walls, hour after hour, and finally collapsed mere feet from one another. She watched them twitch until their bodies gave way into exhausted sleep.

"No!" Alice banged on the glass, knowing it was useless. The foxes would not hear her. If any of the scientists came by, they would haul her away. She slumped to the floor, so numb that she scarcely noticed when her Feed buzzed.

The pigeons, she thought wearily. A slim shimmer of hope rose in her heart. There were footsteps in the hall now and muted but animated chatter as the other scientists responded to the alert. Faintly heartened, she joined the human throng on its eager flight from the building to see the new migration of passenger pigeons.

* * * * *

The sky was overcast, and the day was cool, but Alice scarcely felt it in the heat of the excitement. People were spread everywhere, along the sidewalks, in the parking lot, breathless with anticipation. Even the protestors fell silent as every face lifted toward the sky.

"There!" someone shouted, but there was no need. They appeared like a mist, a mass of birds. An ink spill across the sky. They were a phalanx, a cloud. Thick and fast, and thrilling with life. Around her, dozens of people pointed their Feeds at the sky.

But Alice raised her spirit, as if she might join the birds in the air. She could almost feel the wind, the rush of speed, their trust in something new on the horizon.

Then the first bird fell.

There was an awkward flutter of wings, and the bird tumbled from the flock. It might have gone unnoticed, but several more birds plummeted at the same moment.

Alice heard a gasp. Maybe it was her own.

A moment later, the hail of birds began. Birds plowed into buildings, into the sidewalk. People screamed and ran for cover, their wails punctuated by the staccato smacks of soft bird bodies against the ground. A car alarm erupted when a bird barreled into its hood with a sound like a gunshot.

I should be more surprised, Alice told herself. The initial horror seemed to have broken something inside of her, and she now took in the nightmare with a sort of grim detachment. There would be plenty of time to grieve.

Alice staggered backward into the security of the bus stop shelter. She dragged in a painful breath and pulled the Feed from her pocket. Her voice did not quaver as she uploaded to the Via-Feed "Resurrection" band.

"The passenger pigeon migration has become a mass suicide," she said, and pointed the Feed to take up the images of the dying birds.

Her Feed jolted to life. Others were uploading images onto the Resurrection band—and they weren't just of pigeons, but images that must have been stolen from other Resurrection projects. A bear banging his head against the line of bushes that obscured the bars of its environment. A shark chasing its own tail in a mad spin. Somewhere, she thought she saw an image of Kibwe and Mosi. Was Noura posting?

"Attas" flickered in too—angry faces, clenched fists, howls of rage. Thousands of images and holos, faster and faster. Around her the screaming continued and hundreds of soft bodies slammed wetly into the paved-over world.

A blast struck the shelter, and Alice fell to her knees in fright. She looked up to see a broken pigeon peering down at her though the glass roof above. A patch of red billowed from its body, and she watched its black eye grow dim, like the fire drained out of a diamond.

Her feed was streaming so fast now she couldn't make sense of it. The images froze in a jumble. And in the air, instead of screams of horror, there came a new sound. A howl of anger.

And *that* fanned Alice's flame of hope. Perhaps, after all of the killing and destruction, and even the half-hearted attempt at resurrection, maybe *this* was the moment.

Maybe this was humanity coming back to life.

The Magician's Secret

"Wait! I *love* magic!" Reema plucked Bertrand's shirt and filled a gap in a cluster of people gathering around the street performer.

Bertrand stopped short. It was the first time Reema had expressed unqualified pleasure in anything all day. He'd planned everything, from their lunch at The Flaming Wok (MSG made her ill) to the canoe ride on the lake (the mosquitoes *had* been intolerable, honestly). Their date was, so far, a total fail.

"*I* do magic," said Bertrand, slipping in beside her. "Just some sleight of hand, but I've learned a lot of stuff on YouTube and—"

"Shhh!"

A red satin banner reading "Lorenzo the Magnificent" waved feebly behind the magician who was, at that moment, conjuring coins from the air and dropping them into a fish bowl on a velvet-covered platform. He had black hair and heavy eyebrows over improbably green eyes. Those alone made him magnificent, never mind what his hands were doing.

"He's pretty good," Bertrand whispered, but Reema merely nodded, her eyes trained on Lorenzo's next bit of trickery.

At Lorenzo's direction, an audience member plucked a card from a shuffled deck, signed it "Aziz," and replaced it. Lorenzo shuffled, returned the cards to their box, and set it aside. This done, he took a sealed deck from his jacket, passed it to a woman who broke the seal, spread the cards on the pedestal, and gasped to find the original card, signed in Aziz's distinctive hand.

The audience clapped appreciatively.

"Deck shell, palm, and switch," muttered Bertrand. "That, or Aziz is a plant." A scowling woman gave him a nudge with her elbow. "I didn't tell you *exactly* how he did it," Bertrand grumbled, and he looked up to see Lorenzo observing him with a vague smile.

The next was a particularly pretty piece of magic—pink rose petals conjured in a glass vase and finally rendered as a complete rose. Bertrand wasn't entirely sure how Lorenzo had managed it, but was willing to make a guess. Unfortunately, Reema had moved away from him.

Bertrand felt vindicated, however, when the magician hailed him after the show.

"I'm always happy to see another magician in the crowd," Lorenzo said. "I hope you'll come to my show at the circus tonight." With that, he pulled a "free admission" coupon from behind Bertrand's ear and another from Reema's own hand. "Just remember the magician's code," he said with a dark wink. "We keep one another's secrets."

* * * * *

"Don't tell me how he does anything!" Reema admonished Bertrand as they took their seats amidst the eager crowd. The tent held about one-hundred and fifty audience members, and the benches were lined up directly opposite the stage area. This did not surprise Bertrand, nor did being selected from the audience to join Lorenzo in a disappearing man illusion.

The audience clapped as he rose, and Reema gave a giddy "Ooh!"

No stage platform, so no trap door, Bertrand thought to himself as he made his way forward. *Mirrors, then. Or a hidden panel. That's why Lorenzo invited me here tonight. He knows I'll understand the trick and play along.*

"Thanks for joining me," the magician said with an expansive gesture. "Tell these folks your name."

"Bertrand," he said, warm with pride. He could scarcely make out the audience from the stage. The lights shone brightly on his own face, and the people seated beyond the first two rows were merely human-like shapes in the relative darkness.

"You're not claustrophobic are you, Bertrand?"

"Nope."

"Let's hope not," said the magician, twitching his eyebrows. There was a rumble of amusement from the audience. "If you're sure, go ahead and step right inside of my disappearing box." Lorenzo motioned to the coffin-like apparatus that stood upright between them. "Everybody say good-bye to Bertrand."

Bertrand stepped inside and gave the audience a sudden, anxious expression before looking pointedly at the narrow walls and short ceiling of the box. There were more chuckles from the audience at this, and Lorenzo gave him a conspiratorial wink as he shut the door.

The very last thing Bertrand saw was the faintly illuminated face of Reema where she sat in the front row. She gave him a nod and raised her chocolate ice cream to him in salute. He gave her a finger wave as she disappeared from view.

Bertrand was swallowed into cool darkness, almost blinked out of existence. The silence was so complete that Bertrand couldn't hear his heartbeat, nor even the echo of his breathing off the smothering walls. He expected to hear some direction, but if Lorenzo wanted anything from him, Bertrand had no idea what it was.

Time slithered slowly forward and, were it not for the strange dream-like quality of the experience, Bertrand might have, in fact, begun to feel his first pangs of claustrophobia. But at last, the door swung open, and Bertrand found himself staring out from the box.

"Come out, Bertrand! Welcome back!"

Lorenzo gave a sweep of his cape, and Bertrand staggered forward, squinting in the sudden brightness and feeling woozy and disappointed. The trick had happened without him.

Nevertheless, he took his applause like a good performer should.

"Just between you and me, right?" Lorenzo whispered as they took their bows.

"Definitely."

* * * * *

It gnawed at him—the not knowing. Lorenzo had made him disappear, but Bertrand had no idea how. *He's not* that *good,* he told himself. *What am I missing?*

In addition to the disappointment, Bertrand still felt strangely disembodied. He tried to drown his unease in a large lemonade shared with Reema who, for her part, had shown little interest in his experience in the box. In fact, when Bertrand attempted to broach the subject, she turned on him with, "I told you, I don't want to know!"

Eventually, they grew bored with the carnival attractions and were taking a clandestine tour of the trailer area when Bertrand spied one with "Lorenzo" emblazoned over the door. On impulse, Bertrand made a beeline toward it. He knocked, but there was no response. He tried the door, and it opened smoothly in welcome.

"What are you doing?" Reema hissed, hesitating at a far corner of the trailer. "You can't go in there!"

"I'll be right back," Bertrand assured her, slipping inside.

A lamp in the corner shone on a basic living area with a cluttered table, some seating, a tall cupboard crammed with magic tools, and, to Bertrand's surprise, the disappearing man box.

Now I've got you! he thought gleefully.

Expecting a fake front, Bertrand pulled the door open, only to find it frustratingly solid.

How had it worked then?

Bertrand ran his hand down the facing on both sides of the box. He patted down the walls from the inside and out. He tapped the floor. It seemed to be nothing more than a simple box.

A sudden rap on the side of the trailer nearly rocketed Bertrand from his sneakers, and he peeked out the window to see Lorenzo's approach. Having no alternative, Bertrand slipped into the box, heart racing, and pulled the door to just as the trailer listed with Lorenzo's entry.

Bertrand held his breath, straining to hear what was happening, but as before the box was silent and black as a tomb. How would he ever know when it was safe?

Suddenly, a grating roar ripped through his skull, making his teeth buzz together painfully.

Bertrand threw his arms out in reflex, then jerked them away from the wall, realizing what he was hearing.

Sawing.

Lorenzo was sawing the box.

"Stop!"

But the sawing did not stop.

Bertrand thrust at the door to no avail. The rip of the blade roared again in his ear. Sawdust sifted down onto his shoulder.

"*Stop!*"

Bertrand banged at the walls with fury and kicked the door so hard his toes went numb. The sound merely ricocheted back against his ear drums.

"Let me *out!*"

The saw growled on, and Bertrand's neck began to burn hot and red in the darkness. He felt a viscous trickle down his throat and the pooling of blood against his collar bone.

He dared once to reach up with his hand to find the blade with his finger tips. It felt like certain death. He was blind with panic.

"Stop! *Stop!*"

He pressed his head against the far side of the box, but still the saw bore down on him.

But every time he screamed, the blade bit deeper into that tender skin below his jaw. He fingered his collarbone and patted the sticky wetness there and again felt the slice of the blade.

In desperation, he finally seized the blade, which actually stopped. His fingers burned from the bite of the steel, and Bertrand realized he was crying.

As Bertrand's mind stilled fractionally, he realized the wetness of tears on his cheeks was echoed at his feet. He lifted one foot from the floor experimentally, to understand the sensation. He seized upon it with horror—*his shoes were flooding*. Though he could still see nothing, he could feel the rising water slink up past his ankle bones.

"I'm *in* here!" he screamed.

Bertrand tried to rock the box. He thrust his hips, shoulders, and head, but with every movement, the blade settled more deeply into his neck.

The water rose slowly and resolutely, soaking his socks, filling his shorts. His breath caught as it crept up his chest. Bertrand panted and lifted his face as well as he could. He whimpered as the water crested his chin and trickled into his nostrils. He choked and gagged.

A blast of light shot through Bertrand's brain.

This is the end.

"Come out, Bertrand!"

The door swung open, and the rush of water pulled Bertrand forward. His knees gave and he stumbled into a puddle on the bare ground. He was blind and blinking in the stage lights, scarcely aware of the applause of the audience.

Bertrand flinched as Lorenzo seized his hand and raised it above their heads.

He felt as if he were slowly waking from a bad dream and distantly noted that his clothes were dry.

"Damn good trick, huh?" Lorenzo whispered, giving him a sharp, maniacal smile. "Just between us, right? Magicians keep each other's secrets."

Bertrand didn't manage to bow, and neither did he recall walking back to his seat in the front row. On top of this, his fevered brain could barely make sense of Reema's excited questions. Though he *did* notice that her ice cream was still uneaten.

"That was awesome!" she exclaimed. "Water gushed out the first time he opened the door! But the next time, you were there! How did it work?"

Bertrand could only shake his head in horror-struck wonder, and Reema slapped his leg. "Come on. You *had* to be in on it."

But Bertrand had no voice and could not draw breath to speak, regardless. He knew with certainty that Lorenzo was a far better magician than anyone else in the audience could possibly imagine.

And Reema rolled her eyes and turned back to the performance, never to know what she had missed.

The Pancake Reader

The cyclist at the corner table finger-combed her helmet-flattened hair. Her face gleamed with exertion, and her body was lean and tan. It just figured she'd order the short stack of whole grain pancakes.

Maggie wove her way across the room on aching feet. College in the fall would be a welcome break from the constant waitressing of the summer. But she was fortunate to have a job at all, she told herself, and she ought to be grateful. College was going to be expensive, and she hadn't snared much in the way of scholarships. There weren't exactly a ton of job options in the area either.

The Homestead restaurant hunkered next to a truck stop along Interstate 80, which passed through the endless, muted plains of eastern Wyoming. During her innumerable shifts, Maggie had grown fond of the short-haul truckers, the cowboys ducking in for a bite, and the game-legged stray mongrel out back. But she was weary as well, and now the pancakes were speaking to her.

"Here you go," Maggie said, setting down the plate. "You must be having quite the ride."

"Thirteen miles so far," the cyclist replied. "Need to refuel before heading back," she added, applying a tiny smear of butter to the pancakes and eschewing the syrups. Maggie stared at the streak of shine on the brown-flecked cakes, and recalled the smart-ass adage: *Exercise. Eat right. Die anyway.*

"Life's short," Maggie said with a smile. "You need some maple cream on those, or butter syrup or something."

"Mmm, don't tempt me," the biker said. She regarded the plate now with such a rueful expression that Maggie regretted having said anything.

She felt worse twenty minutes later when a young man stumbled through the door, his voice strident and cracked with fear.

"Help, please! A lady fell off her bike in the parking lot. I think she's dead."

* * * * *

"Poor woman. I heard it was an aneurism." Tara splashed water on her face and rubbed vigorously. The 'Stead's owner, Mr. Ackroyd, hadn't let anyone "brood" after the woman's death the previous day, and had prohibited anyone from speaking of it during work hours. He couldn't monitor the restrooms, though. . . they hoped.

Maggie tidied her ponytail in the mirror and thought of the woman, her sorry, naked pancakes, and her blue bike lying inert on the asphalt.

"Ackroyd said it was a shame. . . that he wouldn't be making more money off of her," she said.

Tara made a nasty sound in her throat. No one liked the Homestead's owner, and Maggie mostly steered clear of him, having been subjected to his "friendly" pats on the backside once too often. He complained about the stray dog that hung about the restaurant and threatened to shoot it some morning. And everyone knew he holed up in his office to chain smoke, which was illegal, and aggravated Tara's asthma. Tara sighed as she dried her face with the rough brown toweling. If anyone worked more hours than Maggie, it was Tara. And she couldn't simply escape to college, having to support herself and a young son.

Tara took a breath, steeling herself, and headed back into the kitchen.

When Maggie picked up the next plate of hotcakes and served it to a tired cowboy, she had an odd impression of romance. He wasn't a handsome fellow. Too lanky, with wide, leafy ears. And he didn't look much like a lover either, but there was something sweet about his hound-dog eyes.

"It's too early to be so blue," she told him.

He shrugged, and blinked down at his coffee cup. "I messed up bad with my girl yesterday. I was an ass. Don't know how to make it up to her."

"You'll think of something," Maggie said, sliding the plate before him. "Pancakes are good for the soul."

A week later, the cowboy's picture appeared on the front page of the paper. He had proposed to his girlfriend by spray-painting his unending love and devotion to her on the Rangeville water tower.

She had said "Yes." *And what girl wouldn't?* The paper rustled in Maggie's shaking hand as she slipped it back into the reading rack.

She was certain now that the pancakes were speaking to her, or rather that she was able to read them, like tea leaves in the bottom of a cup, or rabbit entrails. And not all pancakes spoke to her, but some. A certain smattering of cooked splotches or an undefined shape could indicate a change in wealth, health, business, or relationships. She couldn't ever pinpoint exactly what she was seeing, or when. It was like one of the floaties in your eye that disappears when you try to focus on it, but catches your attention by drifting through your vision when you're not paying attention to anything else.

One morning a young father came in with his tousled-haired toddler. Business was hopping, and Maggie didn't notice the indications of Grave Illness spread across the kiddie stack of blueberry hotcakes until she arrived at their table.

The boy's eyes were wide in anticipation, and he was bouncing in his seat.

"Eat. Eat cakes now!"

"They're coming, buddy. Hang on," his father said, placing a restraining hand on the boy's scrawny shoulder but still beaming down at him.

In desperation, Maggie bobbled the plate which crashed to the floor to the screaming dismay of the toddler.

"I'm so sorry! I'll get you some new ones right away," she said, quickly clearing the mess away. "No, no don't eat that off the floor," she said, brushing the ruined food away from the boy's hand while his father fished him back into the seat.

The boy's second stack of pancakes was silent.

Over the next several weeks, Maggie fumbled more plates, and snuck the occasional flapjack into her apron. She wasn't entirely certain if it was the pancakes themselves that brought the events to pass, or whether they were merely some sort of carbohydrate soothsayers, but Maggie didn't think too much about it either way. She wasn't a philosopher, just a waitress.

Just as there were misfortune cakes there were plenty of good-fortune cakes too, and a couple times Maggie was tempted to take a Wealth cake for herself. Once she served a purple-haired old lady who went and won one thousand dollars on a scratch ticket at the truck stop. Maggie told herself that she had been an important factor in the woman's windfall just to soothe her own envy.

Maggie never ate any of the prophetic cakes, however. In her personal religion of baked goods, she felt that stacking the pancake deck in her own favor would be cheating—and bad juju. She also learned that no one else could read the pancakes. When she asked the cook-staff if they noticed anything strange about a Good Business cake the touchy devils took umbrage. So, Maggie went to Tara, who regarded her with red-rimmed eyes and said, "No, did you drop it? It still looks good enough to serve."

The following Monday Tara didn't show up. "Called in sick," explained Benny, a short-order cook, "Here you'd better take these to Mr. Ackroyd."

"Why?"

"You haven't noticed? Mr. Ackroyd has Tara take him a plate of pancakes every morning at seven sharp. Guess it's your job today."

With a shrug, Maggie took up the plate of buttermilk cakes and a syrup jug and headed for the office. From the other side of the door, Maggie could hear Mr. Ackroyd's smoker's cough, and took a quick look down at the plate.

Huh, a Good Health pancake.

His stinkin' smoking's probably what made Tara sick in the first place, Maggie groused to herself. *He should quit if he wants better health.* And before she could talk herself out of it, Maggie snuck to the back door, gave a short whistle, and watched the stray limp around the side of the building.

The dog was on the small side, but her swinging tail doubled her size. She was mottled brown, with a dusty coat and long, flopping ears.

"Come on, Kelsie girl. Got something for ya." She tossed the pancake toward the dog who wolfed it down and skittered away.

"You're welcome."

Maggie held her breath against the smell of old smoke in Ackroyd's office, and hoped he wouldn't notice the missing pancake. But her boss never even looked at the plate.

"Mmm, looks gooood, girl," he said with a leer.

"Uh, yeah, Benny's pancakes are the best," she said, and scurried from his office.

If Maggie had the slightest regret about redistributing Ackroyd's pancake, that one lascivious gaze snuffed it out.

The next day, Tara called in sick again, and when Benny gave her Ackroyd's plate Maggie saw a Relationship pancake staring up at her.

Ugh.

Was there anyone so unprincipled they could *possibly* deserve a relationship with Mr. Ackroyd?

When Maggie whistled out the back door, Kelsie came at a trot showing no trace of her previous limp. Maggie crouched and coaxed Kelsie forward, and the dog took the treat directly from her hand and accepted a scratch behind her floppy brown ears.

Maggie smiled and did not wash her hands before taking the plate in to Mr. Ackroyd.

"I do love pancakes," he informed her. Maggie tried to hand the plate to him, but he refused to take it, choosing to lean back in his chair which forced her to move in and place it on the desk in front of him. Only then did he incline himself toward Maggie. "You know what else I like?" he breathed at her.

"Decaf?" she said, voice tight. She hurried from the office, ostensibly to fetch the coffee pot, but did not return.

On the third day of Tara's absence, Maggie asked Benny if he couldn't get someone else to take the plate in to Ackroyd, preferably someone capable of growing a beard.

Benny was busy enough for three men, and he didn't catch her meaning or bother to look up from the griddle. "He asked for you specifically," Benny said and banged the order-up bell with the side of his hand.

With a sigh, Maggie picked up her boss's plate and saw a Good Business pancake staring back up at her.

For crying out loud, Maggie thought. *As if Ackroyd could be worthy of it!*

Today Kelsie was waiting at the door and nearly knocked Maggie over with an enthusiastic application of slobber to her hands and neck.

"Good beast," she told the dog.

In his office, Ackroyd proved no less "friendly." His smile gleamed, as did his pomaded comb-over. He rubbed Maggie's shoulders when she served his plate, and he "accidentally" brushed his arm against her chest. Stunned and disgusted, Maggie darted from the room. She spent the rest of the day stumbling through a fog of disbelief and avoiding her boss.

When her shift finally ended, Maggie found Kelsie resting in the shade of her truck, and the dog jumped into the cab when she swung the door open.

Maggie smiled and shook her head, knowing she was helpless to rebuff the affable pooch. "You'll have to learn to ride in the back," she told Kelsie.

The next morning, Maggie had almost persuaded herself to eat a Wealth cake, if it meant she could quit and get away from Ackroyd. But when she arrived at the 'Stead, she found the wait staff looking nervous and speaking in quick, hushed clusters whenever there was a spare moment.

Anxiety gnawed at her as she hurried to the kitchen.

"What's happened? No one's hurt again are they?" Maggie asked Benny, thinking back. She hadn't seen a Pancake-of-Death since the cyclist; had she missed one?

"No, nothing like that," said Benny, flipping an egg. "We just might be out of a job."

"What?" Maggie was stunned. Was this her fault? If she had given Ackroyd the Good Business cake, would that have made a difference?

Benny slid the egg onto a plate with corned beef hash and a slice of toast and passed it over to her. "Tara's brought charges of sexual harassment against Ackroyd. Apparently, she's been helping build a case against him for a while now. Got several other women to join her, too. Even some customers."

He gave Maggie a speculative look, and she turned away to scan the tables and the waiting customers.

"Must be bad, 'cause he got arrested last night," Benny added.

"Damn," breathed Maggie. "I didn't know it was like that."

Benny poured some eggs and pancakes onto the skillet and went back to his work. "I think they ought to throw him under the jailhouse," he said, "but I sure wish I knew what was going to happen here."

Benny didn't have to wait long to find out. The next morning, Maggie arrived to find "Closed" and "Seeking New Ownership" signs posted on the 'Stead. For a moment, Maggie smiled.

Legal fees are a bitch.

Then she felt bad, thinking about all of her co-workers who were now out of a job.

Her spirits dipped even further as, over the next several days, Maggie followed every job lead to a dead end.

About a week after the closing of The 'Stead, Maggie came dragging out from the Kwik Stop, where she had received yet another apologetic, "Sorry, we aren't hiring right now."

She was saved from despair by Kelsie who was always glad to see her. In the back of the truck, she paced back and forth, awaiting Maggie's return, all tongue, happy golden eyes, and sweeping tail.

Maggie stepped up on the back bumper and grabbed Kelsie in a hug that the dog accepted with magnanimity. *"I know you'll have me, at least,"* she said.

"Oh, that's a picture worth a thousand words at least," said a voice behind her, and Maggie half-fell, half-jumped from her perch in surprise.

A man in a crisp blue shirt, charcoal slacks and shiny black shoes stood watching Kelsie with his hands on his hips. *Definitely not from around here,* Maggie thought.

"You look like good friends," he said. "That is your dog, isn't it?"

"Yes, sir. This's Kelsie."

The man scratched Kelsie behind the ears, and her eyes shut in a paroxysm of joy. She had come a long way in just a few days, Maggie thought with satisfaction. The man chuckled and shook his head.

"I'm Evan Duell," he said, extending a card toward her. "I'm a rep for Rocky Mountain Naturals. We're an all-natural pet food business. Maybe you've heard of us?"

"It sounds familiar," she said examining the business card. It wasn't exactly a lie. Maggie had, in fact, heard each of those words before, though not necessarily in that order.

"We've been looking for a new poster dog for our High Country line, and I think Kelsie here . . . I think she might be our ringer."

Maggie was stunned.

She couldn't quite accept all of the unlikely things Mr. Duell was proposing, even as she paraded Kelsie through the parking lot and put her through her newly learned commands.

And Maggie was downright stupefied when, a week later, Mr. Duell returned with a cameraman and photographer, as well as a Rocky Mountain Naturals Deluxe Canine Cabin™, coupons for a lifetime supply of organic kibbles and treats—and a five-thousand dollar check for Maggie.

And so, the Pancake Reader enjoyed her first semester at the University of Wyoming without having to pick up a night shift, and where, every morning, she ate waffles for breakfast.

Frozen Stiff

Parker knew it wasn't right to pout about not having a birthday party this year. He was twelve, after all, not some runny-nosed third-grader. And it wasn't cool for him to be jealous of some old, dead guy. So, Parker just pretended the town was celebrating him, and not the frozen corpse of Ollie Jorgenson.

In spite of the biting cold, a large and enthusiastic crowd cheered as Parker, Mayor Morgan, and Ron the Ice Man took their positions before the TuffShed that was Gran'pa Ollie's crypt.

"Wow, pretty wild!" Parker shouted again to Ron. The Ice Man hadn't heard him the first time; he was going a little deaf.

"You betcha. It's a good crowd!"

Mayor Morgan raised his hands, and the noise quieted enough for his announcement.

"Today is a great day, ladies and gentlemen. Today is Parker Goinseuta's birthday!" This elicited some chuckles and supportive applause, and one enthusiastic whoop. "And to celebrate," the mayor continued, "Parker has been chosen to open this year's Frozen Ollie Fest with the traditional toast in Ollie Jorgenson's memory.

The crowd, gaily festooned in colorful hats, boots, and scarves, cheered yet again. Clouds of breath rose on the frigid air, and Parker watched Ron fumble with his keys and unlock Gran'pa Ollie's specialized coffin.

"Gran'pa Ollie" Jorgenson had been cryogenically frozen upon his death and secreted into a TuffShed in his daughter Martha's back yard nine years prior. When Martha could no longer maintain the costs of keeping Gran'pa Ollie adequately chilled, she revealed her secret and threw herself on the mercy of Rathbone, Wisconsin, which came to the rescue in the form of donations to finance Ron's monthly dry ice delivery and application. The Frozen Ollie Fest was the town's quasi-annual celebration and fundraiser to keep the ice account funded.

Parker's best friend, Myles, had maneuvered his way to the front of the crowd. He gave another whoop and a thumbs-up as Parker raised the lid of Gran'pa Ollie's coffin. A plume of white emerged.

Parker couldn't see much in the coffin—and was glad. Gran'pa Ollie was wrapped in what looked like a thick plastic bag, almost opaque with frost. Parker tore his gaze away before he accidentally saw something memorable, and accepted the cup of hot cocoa from Mayor Morgan.

Parker cleared his throat and raised the cup. "Here's to you, Gran'pa. Thanks for cheering up our long winter."

The toast was short, sweet, and well received. Parker took a sip of the cocoa, burning his taste buds in the process, while Ron raised a Spotted Cow beer (Gran'pa's favorite) to his own lips. Afterward, as the men were closing up, Parker thought he heard a croaking Norwegian voice over the creak of the coffin.

"Get me out of here, boy."

* * * * *

Parker and Myles stood on the iced-over lake watching the Polar Bear Club leap into a bit of open water manned by a laughing EMS team. On the bank, the frozen walleye toss was in full swing, and music from two different stages hovered in the still winter air.

"You gonna join the Polar Bear Club some day?" Myles asked him.

"Uh-uh, looks cold to me," Parker said. They paused to watch a bikini-clad woman scramble breathlessly from the water. "Speaking of cold, do you think he could really come back to life someday?"

"Huh?"

"Gran'pa Ollie got himself frozen in case he could come back to life later on. Do you think it's possible?"

"Maybe."

Myles was not much of a philosopher.

That evening, people were busy drinking and dancing and dressing up for the zombie crawl, so no one noticed when Parker visited the shed, spied the keys that Ron had accidentally dropped in the snow, and slipped inside.

He's frozen, Gran'pa Ollie's definitely frozen solid, Parker told himself. But still he had to make sure.

Holding his breath, Parker pulled open the coffin lid, and a moment later, Ollie Jorgenson tore open his 21st century plastic shroud and sat up.

Parker stumbled back until he hit the wall.

"You—you're alive. But. . . you're frozen!"

Ollie gave an arthritic-looking shrug.

"Wall, it seemed like a good idea at the time, yanno."

"F-freezing yourself?" Parker's lips were numb with shock.

"I didn't figure it'd be much different than sitting in an ice fishin' shack," said Gran'pa. "And I always liked that." He heaved himself from the frozen coffin and hit the floor with a grunt.

"Wait, where are you going?"

"Out!" Gran'pa pulled the shed door open and paused to take in his first look at a new world. "Wall, would you look a'that!" he hooted. Gran'pa shook his head with wonder as two staggering corpses lumbered across their line of sight. Miserable groans, carried by a thin breeze, slithered into the open shed, and Ollie threw his head back and laughed.

The zombie crawl had begun.

"Come back!" Parker cried. But Ollie had already bolted from his steel tomb, intent on joining a dozen groaning "zombies" lurching down the road.

There would have been worse days to accidentally release Gran'pa, Parker admitted as he jogged along beside him. Ollie's hoarse groans and laughter blended in perfectly with the wild noise of the crowd.

A woman with dreadlocks and gruesome face paint glanced over at Ollie and shuddered.

"Wow. Great make-up. You really look dead," she said with a compulsive smile.

"Thanks!" Ollie gave her a stiff thumbs-up, and the woman drifted away and disappeared into the crowd.

In the center of town, people were cheering outside the shops as the zombie apocalypse descended. Parker hung near to Gran'pa, not knowing what else to do, but feeling weirdly of place.

"You're not a zombie," some spectator jeered.

"Eat him! Eat his brains out!" someone yelled. And Ollie pretended to grab fistfuls of Parker's head and cram them into his mouth. He gobbled noisily, and the crowd roared.

"You can't do this!" Parker hissed at him.

"You see that I can," Ollie said with a laugh. "Ohh! Coffee! Coffee break!"

"I don't think that's a good idea!" cried Parker.

But Gran'pa, who had really limbered up now, was already striding away toward the coffee shop.

"Coffee, please," he said to the barrista.

"Tall, grande, or venti?"

"Black decaf is good enough for me."

She pointed to the cups. "Which size?"

"Oh." He blinked. "I want the big one." The girl filled an enormous cup with coffee and carefully worked a lid on top. Ollie patted his pocket as she rang him up.

"I got it," Parker whispered to him, fishing in his pocket for some crumpled bills. But the girl's eyes never veered from Ollie as she made change.

"I've served a lot of dead guys today. But you take the cake," she said.

"Good to hear," said Ollie, pleasantly.

As Gran'pa took the cup, Parker noticed that his hand had lost its dusting of white, revealing the green-grey beneath. It was a color that said, *Yep, dead.*

Gran'pa sniffed his drink, frowning as they left the shop. "Four dollars, and it doesn't even smell like anything." He gave a tentative taste, then another one. Then a longer pull, until coffee dribbled from the corner of his mouth and hit the salted sidewalk underfoot.

"Your lips," Parker gasped. "They're melting, er— thawing!"

Ollie pressed his gray fingers to his mouth in horror.

"You've gotta go back!" shouted Parker.

"No!"

Ollie dropped the cup and dashed through the crowd and toward the wooded park with Parker in pursuit.

"Come back!" Parker hollered after him.

He moves fast for an old, dead guy, Parker thought. They crunched through the snow, Gran'pa charging ahead with Parker in full pursuit, over dead branches, and through a maze of denuded oaks. Parker pumped his arms and huffed till his lungs burned. Finally, Gran'pa stumbled. Parker thought it was the end, but the old man pressed on with an awkward, lumbering gait.

Parker paused to collect the boot left in the snow, peered inside, and grimaced.

"Your foot fell off! Gran'pa!" Parker called. He held up the boot, and Gran'pa looked back at it forlornly, then down at his empty pant leg.

When Parker caught up with him, Ollie was seated on a fallen tree, head nodding like he was falling asleep. He gave a sad sniff and wiped his nose on his sleeve. An important part of his face went with it, and Parker blinked away.

"Wall, I can't stay after all, I guess," Ollie said, "but I don't wanna freeze any more either. Can't a man change his mind?"

Not after they die. Not in general, thought Parker.

"I promise you won't have to freeze. But, you do have to go back."

Gran'pa sighed. Dead though he might be, he was wise enough to accept the inevitable, but human enough to regret it.

So, the two made their way back to the TuffShed. Parker threw the dry ice out of Gran'pa's coffin with Ron's hand shovel while Gran'pa pitched it out with his bare hands.

With a groan, Ollie managed to lever himself back inside, and Parker snuck Gran'pa's boot into the leg of his overalls. The old fellow had grown a little too soft and tired to manage it himself.

He sagged back into the coffin with a sigh.

"It was a pretty good night, yanno? I got to get out one more time and shake out the bones. Not everyone gets that."

"That's true," Parker said.

"How old are you, boy?"

"It's my birthday; I'm twelve. And my name is Parker."

"Wall, happy birthday, Parker. And many more."

At that, the old man's eyes closed and the green-grey lips settled in a well-meaning, though still disturbing, smile and moved no more.

Parker closed the lid to Gran'pa's coffin, locked the TuffShed behind him, and pocketed the keys, just in case.

And that was the last year of the quasi-annual Frozen Ollie Fest.

The TuffShed cryogenics crypt was abandoned and Gran'pa Ollie was reduced to ashes. His granddaughter sprinkled him in the waters of Oahu for a change of scenery.

"Maybe he'd had enough of the cold."

Those were his granddaughter's exact words as immortalized in the *Rathbone Gazette*.

Reading them, Parker grinned and thought, *You don't know just how right you are.*

"Frozen Stiff" was inspired by the hugely entertaining "Frozen Dead Guy Days" celebration in Nederland, Colorado. Much like "Gran'pa Ollie," Nederland's "Grandpa Bredo" is cryogenically frozen and maintained in a TuffShed kept sufficiently cold with a monthly delivery of a ton of dry ice. Psychics report that Grandpa Bredo is pleased that his memory brings so much joy to festival participants.

Perchance to Dream

As of this morning, it's been four hundred and seventy-seven days since I last slept. In the interest of full disclosure, I'm counting from the last hour of sleep I actually had, not from the first hour of sleep I missed, which is how most people count it.

It's winter now and overcast, with dusk settling in extra early, and I find myself hoping, as I do every day at this time, *Please, let me sleep tonight.*

I shouldn't complain. The oldest living Wakist, Raul Lago, has gone without sleep for twenty-nine years now—thirty next month. There's a big celebration being planned for him down in São Paulo, and the powers-that-be are determined he make it that long. Rumor has it he's been on suicide watch for the last two years.

When his condition was first recognized, he was hailed as an evolutionary advancement. A fourteen-year-old human who didn't need sleep and was never physically exhausted. Incredible! (I was sixteen when I lost sleep, and by that time Wakism was credible enough to be dreaded by anyone with a lick of sense.)

A full fourteen percent of the world population is believed to be Wakist now, and the suicide rate is through the roof. Keeping Señor Lago around is supposed to give the rest of us hope and inspiration.

The problem is, you see, that sleep is more than just a rest for the body. It gives the brain a chance to recuperate, to hide away a bit from the challenges of waking life. We dream—those who still can, I mean—to sift through ideas and problems of the day and repair our nervous systems. Lack of sleep can lead to impairments in memory and problem solving and speech. Throw in some depression on top of that, and you can see why we're not a lot of fun.

A lot of Wakists suffer from what's colloquially referred to as "Wakeheimers", a disorder caused by brain exhaustion. Some people forget who they are, where they live. Others repeat themselves over and over again because they don't remember they've said it all before. But I think sometimes it's just that we have so much time now, and relatively little to say. That's one more perk of slumber, it keeps you from having to fill empty space with idle chit-chat.

There were quarantines, of course, when Wakeheimers was first identified, but those days are long gone. There were Wakists all over the world by that time, cases appearing by the thousands each month, occurring spontaneously, as far as scientists can determine. No one knows what causes it. It's not viral, or bacterial, or genetic. Some people think it's related to cell phone waves or satellite frequencies, yet other people claim it stems from toxins in the environment. Others insist it's some sort of extra-terrestrial experiment. Still *others* say that this is the judgment from some sadistic-slash-"all-loving" deity. But I don't believe in God at all anymore, not since Mom got Wakeheimers.

Dad left a couple years before Mom started showing signs of Wakeheimers, but he claimed they didn't have enough in common once she could no longer sleep, and that was a deal-breaker for him. But we did okay on our own because Mom taught at Armstrong Prep. She was one of the really good teachers whose night classes were as full as her day ones. You see, once Wakism really set in, adults began working more and taking on night shifts just to have something to do, and plenty of Wakist kids started schooling "after hours" too.

That's how I met Ivan. It was the first week of spring night-mester and he was walking around Armstrong looking for room D306, where Mom's world literature class was being held, and trying to avoid the unmanly necessity of asking directions. His parents kicked him out when he lost sleep, and he was hitching from town to town, looking for something to keep him out of a home for abandoned Wakist kids.

I liked him immediately, from his sheepish smile, to the silly little bow he made when I offered to show him the way to class. Mom liked him too, for three whole months—until the day she didn't recognize him at all. I remember the exact moment because she gave him one of those friendly smiles reserved for strangers. I managed to drop his name and insinuate that he was my boyfriend, and she shot me an embarrassed smile when Ivan's back was turned. Lots of people muddle through for a long time with Wakeheimers, but by the end of the next week, when Mom started explaining pathos vs. logos for the third time in five minutes, I helped her out of the classroom and back home. The week after that, there were times she couldn't even recognize *me*.

By the end of the month, Mama had just enough of her wits about her (if you could think of it that way) to fill her pockets with rocks and walk into Marvine Lake. She left a note for me, so I knew where to send the search and rescue people.

I'm grateful she chose drowning, I guess, so I didn't have to be the one to find her— bleeding or bulging or blue. She could have gone to a clinic, too. There's one in our city. People come from miles away, even crossing state borders, to be eased into eternal sleep.

There are picketers there on most days. But there are other people who escort families through the doors, knowing full well they'll be seeing fewer numbers pass back the same way. Lots of times those escorts have family members who didn't choose distant drowning, but something more immediate—and traumatizing.

Rest without fear. That's their motto.

Anyway, I'm not really surprised Mama went out the way she did. There was a famous writer who committed suicide by water-walk, but I can't remember who. Maybe I'll look it up someday.

As for me, I'm not a suicide. No way.

A lot of people came to the funeral. I sniffled and wept and fielded hugs from probably a hundred people. Students, former students, and teachers—plenty of people I didn't even know, but maybe I looked so pathetic it brought out the touchy-feely in all of them.

The funeral was pretty simple, but I did have Pastor Keri officiate. She did a good job, mostly inviting people up to talk about my Mom and share memories, and not too much Bible stuff. She did come to me afterward, in the foyer, asking me if I wanted her help with legal stuff and papers, seeing as I was an abandoned/orphaned minor, or whatever. I was glad to accept and practically snotted and sobbed all over myself. It had been a hard day. Then she started telling me that even though I was going through a tough time in my life that God understood and he was grieving right alongside of me. And I got angry.

That was crap, and I told her so. It was Ivan who was grieving with me. The people who hugged me were the people who were grieving with me. If there was a God, it was a dirty villain, and I didn't want anything from it. I was screaming now, scarcely able to stand upright, and Ivan pulled my arm over his shoulder and dragged me from the church as I stumbled along blind and raving.

I don't want you to imagine that Wakists are all a bunch of heathens now, just because *my* faith failed. A whole crop of crazy, new beliefs has sprung up in the last several years. At first lots of Wakists just pursued hedonism. There's more time for drinking and dancing and other nighttime amusements when you don't have to sleep, after all. The Department of Health actually encouraged "safe-sex-a-thons." "Orgasm releases melatonin, a natural sleeping agent!" the PSAs announced. And for a while the Catholic Church even joined the Evangelicals in referring to Wakists as the "Sleepless Sinners"—until the Pope joined our ranks.

Now, there's been a big population boom in the US, mostly among teens, and the traditional religionists blame the DOH and the sex-a-thons for this. But seeing as how both euthanasia *and* abortion clinics are so popular these days, you wouldn't think I'd get the evil eye as often as I do when pushing the stroller down the sidewalk. Yeah, I'm young, but I do my best to be a good mom. Ivan and I chose to keep our baby; I think we were trying to make up for missing our own families a little.

I'll never forget the look on Ivan's face when I told him I was pregnant. I'd stayed home from school that day because I was feeling sick, and by the time he'd come home, I'd figured out why.

Ivan went still as a statue, and then a strange drama of emotions flittered across his face as if someone were thumbing slowly through an old cartoon flipbook. Eyes glazed, he eased himself into a dining chair, and when he finally looked up at me, his face displayed a sort of terrified reverence.

"We're going to keep it, right?"

I hadn't been certain, but when he said that, I knew for sure we were going to keep our baby. The idea of being a father lit a sudden fire under Ivan, and he began making plans.

"I'll just get my GED instead of finishing up this year," he told me, pacing the kitchen. "And I'll start trade school next term instead. And loans. I need to look at school loans. We need to get some better money coming in."

We had my mom's Social Security, but Ivan said that was just for me. He wanted to take care of his family.

I got bigger and kept going to school, and my teachers all tried to support me, but I wished Mom were there. I missed her so much, and sometimes, I'd go to the bathroom in the middle of the night so I could cry and not distract Ivan from his online studies.

As our baby's arrival got closer, we had more and more questions.

I wonder what birthing will be like.

I wonder who she'll look like.

I wonder if she'll want a pet someday.

And, the most important question of all.

I wonder if she'll sleep.

People told me I'd probably get religious again after Charlotte was born, but I haven't. Ivan's joined a group, though. Every night they gather together in the park, rain or shine, and lie down with pillows and blankets and perform unison yawning and meditation. It's not really fun, or even restful, Ivan says, but he's convinced that synchronized yawning may help counter the "restless waves" and may restore the balance between sleep and wakefulness to humanity.

I tell him how stupid this is and point out the inconvenient reality of time zones. "All of your meditation vibes are just being counteracted by a rickshaw puller working his ass off on the other side of the world," I explain. "He's running through the streets, while you're yawning for a better tomorrow."

I blame the Yawners group for our breakup, but I guess it was really me. I never learned to keep my mouth shut.

Ivan's jaw tightens whenever I criticize, but he doesn't blow up. Not since he left. "I don't see you doing anything to help," he says. "And I'm tired of explaining it to you. Besides, you haven't gone sleepless as long as I have." Maybe he has a point.

I wonder how it is for people who have never known sleep at all, how beautiful it would be to not know what you're missing. Like our little Charlotte. She's five months old with apricot cheeks, feathery hair and whisky-colored eyes that have never closed for longer than it takes to blink or wail in infant fury.

I held them shut once, just to get a better look at those fragile lavender-threaded lids—at least that's what I tell myself. She fussed and then she screamed, and she fought until I had to brace her head between my knees and block her scratching hands away with my elbows. I let her go when I heard my neighbor coming down to check on us.

I felt horrible afterward, totally sick with myself. I love her so much, and I would never, ever hurt her. But sometimes the craziest things pop into my head.

I need to get away from her sometimes, and get her away from me. That's another thing sleep is for: escape. From obligation. Other people. The oppression of your own waking thoughts.

"Hell is other people," someone said once. And that's true. I've started collecting rocks, and I found a pair of pants with big, deep pockets. If I ever need a permanent break from people, I plan on walking into the river. Mom would understand.

Anyway, it's a good thing Ivan's going to take Charlotte tonight. I don't remember exactly what time he said he'd be by, before Yawners, I hope. I *hope*. He's a good father, and I'm glad for that.

It *is* tonight he's coming, isn't it?

It's dreaming I miss the most, I think. Slipping into that personal theatre where anything is possible, and nothing is predictable, and all responsibility has vanished. Every day, people should have that freedom; that's what dreams are good for.

Did I mention that as of this morning it's been four hundred and seventy-seven days since I last slept? In the interest of full disclosure, I am counting from the last hour of sleep I got, and not the first hour of sleep I actually missed.

Dusk is falling, hushed and heavy now, and I'm hoping, as I always do when the sunlight fades, Oh, *please*, let it be tonight.

Nifty

Raju had heard it said that Boulder, Colorado, was ten square miles surrounded by reality. He thought that was funny, and probably true, and no place made that more true than Pearl Street Mall. Raju spent many happy afternoons walking the bustling, pedestrian street mall and darting from weirdo to weirdo. He soaked up the street performers, raving evangelists, and bleary-eyed bums with a hungry curiosity while his babysitter played footsie—and handsy, and everything else she and her boyfriend could get away with—in Eva's Hemp House and Bakery.

Like any devotee of the arts, Raju had his favorite performers. He cheered for the knife-juggling unicycle rider, and he adored the freckled woman who could throw playing cards onto the roofs of distant buildings. Raju also felt a special kinship to the skinny black man with the braids who could fold himself into a tiny box and had, one time, asked Raju to close the lid. (He looked like Raju's uncle, Aadi, except Taya Aadi couldn't even touch his toes.)

But as much as Raju admired these talents, he coveted them, too. He wanted to do something peculiar and special, something to make people stop and watch, even if they didn't give him their pocket change. He ran through his repertoire, watching himself in the display window of Molly's Shooz. He wiggled his ears, touched his tongue to the tip of his nose, then did a handstand for six seconds.

In the reflection, Raju noticed two college-aged kids; the boy, with a University of Colorado cap, watched him with an amused expression. The girl on his arm gave Raju a friendly grin and they moved on, but they didn't really look impressed.

'Cause I'm really not that impressive, Raju admitted to himself, brushing the dirt from his hands.

"Would you like to do something important and see something to amaze you?"

The voice came from just over his shoulder, and Raju started. He turned quickly to find a short woman next to him, standing a little too close. Raju stepped back, to get a full view.

She was the happy, plump shape of a grandmother who liked baking cookies, but her face was young. Her lavender-colored hair was shot with white and fell in tight spirals to her waist.

And her eyes were silver.

Raju was already amazed just looking at her. "Did you say something?" he finally croaked.

"I've been watching you. You like the performers. You understand them."

"They're. . . nifty," he said, staring hard.

"Yes, well, you seem to be a student of the nifties," she said. "And we need an expert to judge. Quickly. Will you come?"

"To judge. . . nifties? Performers?"

The woman nodded. "Yes, very good. Judge the nifties. Quickly now." Suddenly, there was a door in the brick wall where there had been no door a moment before. The woman pulled the handle and passed through. Raju hesitated.

"Quickly," she repeated, descending the stairs on the other side.

With a last, quick look back to the street, and knowing this was the wrong thing to do, Raju followed her down. The walls were sketched with white light, and he felt something like a fly trapped in a web.

By the time he hit the landing, Raju intended to turn and trot right back up, but he stopped short. There, in a well-lit room, were two monsters.

Raju's legs nearly went out from under him.

One monster was an enormous slug-shape covered with fur. He had ears like a wolf and, instead of arms, six furry tentacles hung on either side of his body. Most curiously, the monster's face resembled a seal with a small twitching nose and bristling whiskers. His black beseeching eyes were as round as super balls.

The other creature was not quite as tall as Raju. A bulbous caterpillar creature on dozens of stilt-like praying mantis legs. He was translucent green with blue and red markings. Two stumpy antennae poked up from his head above his beady eyes and slit of a mouth.

"They are nifty, are they not?" The woman smiled at him, but Raju was frozen. He tried to nod, but found his head fixed.

The furry beast opened its mouth and roared so loudly that Raju thought he could see the disturbance in the air around him. "Ahh!" He clutched the woman reflexively. She felt sticky, like new tar on a hot road.

"He is afraid, Tnef," the woman said, "Back off, now." The woman snapped her fingers, and the caterpillar came clattering over, his tiny feet clickety-clackety on the stone floor. As Raju watched, thin white cords spooled out from the creature's antennae and toward Raju, who cringed hard against the sticky woman.

"Do not be 'fraid," she said. "It won't hurt."

It was impossible to not be afraid, and Raju bit his lips and quaked when the antennae dipped into either ear—but not from pain, from the tickle. His ears suddenly felt very full and they popped, the way they did when he went down in an airplane. Then, a warm webby feeling sparkled through his brain. He shivered and clutched the woman more tightly, and she rubbed his hair.

Then, the sensations in his head stopped, and Raju cracked one eye open.

The furry beast was watching him thoughtfully with his stunned seal-face.

"Do you understand me now?" he said.

Raju swallowed. "I-I understand you," he croaked.

"So, you can do something? You show us?" asked the caterpillar, antennae twitching.

Raju didn't know what was expected, but if this were some sort of performance, he felt he'd better come up with something. Raju slowly peeled himself away from the sticky woman, and, in spite of the shock that made his body feel very stiff, he stuck his tongue out, wiggled his ears, and briefly stood on his hands. He only managed a couple of seconds because his arms felt very weak.

The caterpillar made a wet bubbly sound of affirmation.

"And he's human, too," said the woman.

"Good. He will be a good judge," the beast said.

Raju cleared his throat. "I think he wins." He glanced quickly at the caterpillar. "I mean, you're all. . . very interesting, but. . ."

"Not us," said the caterpillar in his gurgly way. "Those." He pointed with his antennae.

In the corner, where Raju hadn't noticed them before, stood three street performers. They appeared to be frozen in place. They all stared straight back at Raju like they were in some sort of line-up. One man had brightly dyed orange hair streaked with red and black, like flame. The other had no hair at all, but small horn implants on his bald head, large gauges in his ears, and tattoo sleeves down his arms and around his neck. The third man was tall and skinny. He had a white face, pale bulging eyes, and corn silk hair. He looked like someone had just poured him out of a milk jug.

"Humans," said Raju.

The caterpillar made a disappointed sound. "In fact, one is *not* human. One is the Draconath and you must tell what one he is."

"The Draconath can take on forms very well, but not perfectly. When he goes to a new planet he takes on the form of one of their nifties," said the woman. "Doing this, he can hide his mistakes more easily, and the creatures of the planet don't even notice. It is unfortunate for you that he has chosen Earth this time, of course."

"Why is it unfortunate?" Raju asked.

"Draconath buries many fire seeds in the planets. Then they hatch. All hatch to make more Draconath, and planet explose into many pieces. Big explose, very little pieces. Planet gone then. Very sad," said the caterpillar with a woeful gurgle. "You know my meaning?"

"We have been chasing him for a long time, and he knew we were near, and that he could not get away. So he has shared himself, just a little bit of essence, inside some humans. A disguise," added the woman. "Now we don't know which one he truly, and we can only take one of them. It is the way."

"It is the way," the others agreed in thoughtful unison.

Raju's head was swimming. "So, you want me to identify the. . . not-human? Because it's an outer-space mega-wasp whose babies will blow up the Earth?"

"Correct," the beast said pleasantly.

"You must do it soon, and you must be certain. As soon as you decide, we will take him and have him disintegrated, and his fire seeds will die. He will then expand as the universe expands until he can not come back together. It is the best way."

"Does it hurt?"

"It hurts very much," said the beast. "But not for long, only until all his essence is fully scattered. Maybe twelve years your earth time."

"Is too good for Draconath. He deserves Inzorfinator," the caterpillar muttered, and the beast nodded somberly.

Raju didn't know what the Inzorfinator was, but it didn't sound too good. The woman scowled and her silver eyes glittered.

"We've have talked about this before. This is the right way," she chided, and the caterpillar's antennae wilted. "I can only hold him here for a short time," said the woman. The lights in the walls flickered faintly. "I have only a few minutes left. Soon he will be able to decellulize himself here and recellulize himself somewhere else in the galaxy, and we must follow. Shortly after that, your planet will be gone. So, you must choose before my strength gives out, and we will take the Draconath away."

Raju was stung. "What if I can't? Or I choose wrong, you're just going to leave? You can't . . . save us?" *Save me,* the darkest part of Raju wanted to say.

"We must follow Draconath. And explosing will not hurt so much. Big confusion. Very fast. Then, all done," said the caterpillar. "But is sad for us when you are gone."

"Very fast, that's good," Raju muttered. "Plus at least I won't know if I've accidentally sent an innocent guy to be uncellu—whatevered."

"Yes," agreed the beast. "And also, if you mistake him, the Draconath will surely destroy more planets before we can find him again."

Raju shriveled under the burden.

"What if I want someone else to do it?"

"Too short time now. You must do," said the caterpillar.

Raju sighed. The earth was going to explose, and his correct choice would be the only thing to stop it.

"I'll do my best," he said.

"Very good," said the woman. "He will judge you!" she announced to the three men, who suddenly came to life before Raju's eyes. They started and blinked and looked all around them.

"What did you do to us? What the hell's going on?" bellowed the tattooed man, starting forward. The beast gave a roar, and the man scurried back to stand with the others. The orange-haired guy scratched the back of his head.

"Is this so we can get a busking license?" he asked.

"You will do everything this boy says," replied the woman, ignoring his question. "Quickly," she said to Raju again.

"I-I need to ask you all some questions, I guess," Raju said, unsure how to explain himself. "What do you do?" he asked the orange-haired man, who never took his eyes from the monsters as he answered.

"I'm a fire eater."

"I've never seen you around here before."

"I'm from Chicago. Just got in yesterday; I'm scoping out the place. That's why I don't have my gear today."

"Aren't you kinda young to be a fire-eater?"

The man snorted disdainfully. "Kid, there's no age requirement. Just a consistent lack of parental supervision." He snorted at his own joke.

That sounded pretty human. Would aliens know about parental supervision? Or Chicago?

He looked to the tattooed man with the horns.

"I've seen you, but I don't really know what you do." Raju didn't love the body artists. Seeing tattoos made his flesh prickle.

The tattooed man replied, "I don't need gear. Listen to this." He puckered his lips and began to whistle. It was a little weak because the man was trembling, but Raju recognized the melody immediately. Beethoven's Fifth Symphony. It was incredible, spot-on and musical in a way he didn't know whistling could be.

"That's amazing," he said, cutting the man off sooner than he would have liked.

"I sing opera and do bird calls too." Suddenly, Raju thought there was a seagull somewhere in the room; he scanned the ceiling before realizing his mistake. The tattooed man was grinning with the corner of his mouth.

"Dang. I didn't expect that," said Raju.

"That's part of the point. Most people expect. . . well, who knows what they expect," he said, shrugging a massive, tattooed shoulder.

The last man, the one with the bulbous eyes, and wispy hair, watched the interviews with a worried expression.

"What do you do?" Raju asked him.

"I'm a body artist. I'm Bendit."

"Show me."

The man sighed. "I'm not warmed up. It's cold down here, but I'll try." He rolled his head on his neck, and it cracked ominously.

Without any obvious effort, he then leaned into a back fold and lowered it to a chest stand. In this position, the man was on his belly with his butt bent up over his head, and his feet on the floor in front of his face. He reminded Raju of a flexistraw.

"That's pretty good," said Raju, who had seen the like before, but wanted to be kind.

The man shrugged a knobby shoulder. "It seems a bit boring right about now, frankly. You know, compared with. . ." He jutted his chin toward the aliens.

Raju snorted. "Yeah, I know."

"How long?" said the caterpillar. "You must choose soon."

Raju looked hard at the performers. How could he tell which was human? What did humans do that made them different from other creatures?"

"What's your favorite drink?" he asked.

"Beer, kid," said the tattooed man.

"Coke," said the fire eater.

"Green tea," answered the contortionist.

All reasonable, Raju thought. "Fast food?"

"Chipotles," said the fire eater

"Uh, me too. Chipotles," said the contortionist.

"McDonalds's," said the tattooed man.

Hmm.

Strike against the contortionist for not coming up with his own restaurant. And a strike against the tattooed man too. Did any human being like McDonalds best?

The fire-eater was tapping his foot impatiently, he gave a glance at the aliens and set his jaw.

"Move aside. I'm outta here," he said, shouldering his way past Raju and toward the door.

There was a blur of brown fur as beast moved faster than Raju could have imagined. He slid over on his snail belly and poked the fire eater with a tentacle.

A yelp echoed off the walls and the fire-eater disappeared. Where there had been a man a moment before, there was now a puddle of skin on the floor. It pooled out from the clothes and its edges were fringed with fingers and toes, while the brown eyeballs pointed in different directions near a thatch of greasy hair.

The contortionist screamed and the tattooed man cowered.

"Put him back, now!" the woman barked.

Just as quickly the skin filled back up, and the fire eater stood before them again, his wide eyes watching in mute horror.

"You all stay now and do as judge says," the caterpillar snapped. "You understand?"

Three heads nodded.

"You must hurry!" the woman said to Raju.

What else? He demanded of himself.

"Hold out your hands!"

The men did so, and rapidly. Raju felt each one of them. All human—tendons and skin and bones. The contortionist's hands felt colder, and more wobbly. *But still human, I think.*

"What was your favorite TV show as a kid?" he asked.

"We didn't have TV," said the tattooed man. "My parents thought it was a bad influence."

"SpongeBob," said the contortionist.

"The Simpsons."

Ok, no TV was weird, but not impossible.

Raju turned to the woman. "Are you *sure* it's one of these guys?"

"We know with certainty. We can feel the essence."

"Boy maybe not good choice," the caterpillar muttered.

Raju ground his teeth.

"Who was your thirteenth grade teacher?"

"There is no thirteenth grade," sniffed the contortionist. "Oh, that was a trick, huh? Nevermind."

Raju snorted. It had been a trick, as the contortionist pointed out. Did that make him less human or more human? Raju didn't know.

"One minute left," said the woman.

The beast made an impatient sound.

"I'm thinking. I'm *thinking*!" said Raju. How was he supposed to think? Three terrified men in front of him. Strange alien creatures practically breathing down his neck. He looked from one to another, and suddenly inspiration struck.

"Take off your clothes!" he shouted at the performers. "Take them off now!"

"Ten seconds."

"What? You're kidding," said the contortionist. His white skin flushed in an instant.

"Dude, that's a chick," the tattooed man said, squinting at the lavender-haired alien. "At least, I think it is. And what if someone comes down here?"

"If someone comes down here, we're going to have a lot more explaining to do than why we're butt naked below the street," the fire-breather said, unhappily pulling up his shirt.

"Five."

Raju scampered back, bumping into the furry beast.

"That one," he whispered.

"You are sure?"

"Yes."

No. Not exactly. But it was the best he had with —"Three" – seconds left.

"Him!"

The caterpillar's antennae lashed out like whips and encircled the fire eater in a flash. The woman raised her arms, and a crash of air like thunder filled the room as the beast bellowed. The lights throbbed blinding white and Raju covered his eyes with his arm.

"No!" the fire eater screamed as the light faded. He shook and steamed and in a moment appeared as an enormous worm, covered in frog bumps and mouths. Each mouth was sprinkled with broken teeth and howled in anger. He began to inflate like a balloon. Slowly, slowly, as large as a sewer pipe now. The mouths made a sick gnashing sound.

"Now, you shall be punished, Dragonath!" growled the beast.

The Draconath explosed in a loud bang. Fragments flew in all directions. Raju ducked, but the pieces disappeared before hitting anything at all. As he slowly collected his bearings again, Raju noticed that the contortionist's pants had a wet patch on the front. He hoped his weren't in a similar state, but he could scarcely feel anything beyond the shaking of his own body. The pale man screamed and ran away, followed by the tattooed whistler who slunk along the wall, never taking his eyes off of Raju and the aliens, until he turned to make a quick sprint for the stairs.

"No worry for them," the beast told Raju, watching the men disappear above. "All Dragonath essence gone now."

"You were marvelous!" the woman cried, clasping Raju in a quick embrace. "The Dragonath is gone and his fire seeds will die."

"How did you know him?" asked the caterpillar.

Raju swallowed, trying to recover himself. "Well, he was the only one who didn't seem embarrassed about taking off his clothes. I guess if it's not really your kind of body, you don't have the same feelings about it." Raju knew he'd have stripped down too, if being a puddle were the alternative—but he'd have made a feeble protest first.

"Yes, I think you are right," the woman said with a nod.

The beast grunted. "Your kind are safe, for now, and so are many others. We are grateful to you."

"Thank *you*," said Raju. "You're the ones who sent him away."

"Well, he get now what he deserve," said the beast.

The caterpillar sniffed his disagreement, and asked Raju, "So, you like nifty, yes? You watch them very much."

"Yeah. They're cool I guess."

"But you want to be nifty, too? Yes? Maybe a little?"

Raju gave a half shrug. He'd just saved the whole world and met aliens from another galaxy; being a "nifty" seemed like a very small thing now. "It'd be all right," he said.

The beast slid a friendly, warm tentacle over his shoulder. "Maybe we help you some for that."

* * * * *

"No way!"

"How are you doing that?"

Raju grinned at the crowd of kids pressing toward him to get a better look.

"Do it again!"

He gave a sigh, as if scarcely enjoying the attention, and poked his tongue out again, turning his head in all directions for everyone to get a better look.

"It's blue this time," gasped a girl.

An older man cackled through his beard.

"Can you do rainbow?" asked a boy.

"Polka dots!"

"Plaid," suggested a woman with a toddler strapped to her back.

Raju took her up on it, and this time, his tongue was cross-hatched with red, yellow, and black. The audience applauded enthusiastically.

"That's really quite a trick."

"How do you do it?"

Raju pinched his lips together. "Can't tell you."

"'Cause then you'd have to kill us, huh?" said a mohawked girl.

Raju quirked an eyebrow at her, and the girl laughed nervously.

Raju closed his performance by poking his tongue out one more time and revealing his original pink-brown wiggler and taking a bow. This, too, earned him a warm rain of applause.

And that's all I need, thought Raju. Tips were beside the point now. Because while having a color-changing tongue wasn't exactly a talent, it was still pretty nifty.

Saved

The tiny green and blue sphere floated in the star-flecked expanse of darkness. It was singularly vivid, the fervent mixture of colors so rare outside of forming star clusters and nebulae that it took Nakia's breath away. She hadn't expected to see it again; the Ancients believed the Destruction was several more eras away, but things had taken a bad turn and evacuation was necessary. Now. And not everyone could be taken in.

Nakia felt Rafeen approach to observe the planet from behind her. They stood in silence for a few minutes, the faint hum of the ship's engine lulling them into a dreamy state as the tiny planet grew in the window. Nakia found her voice first.

"They just reach a certain stage of development and rot completely, don't they?" Hearing the pain in her words, Rafeen slid an arm around her waist and leaned his cheek against her hair. "It's just so beautiful," Nakia whispered.

"And it will be again. After the Destruction, the Resurrection," he said.

"But it won't be the same. Not anywhere close. And not for a very long time."

Rafeen nodded in agreement. It would be millions and millions of years, very likely, before the colorful planet was anything like it appeared now. Long after Nakia and Rafeen and all the children of the Ancients had gone back to stardust.

Nakia suffered an almost irresistible urge to reach out toward the poor, primitive little planet. "They don't even appreciate what they have," she said.

"They just don't realize how rare it is."

"You're sticking up for them?"

"No. . . ." But he was a little bit, excusing them. Not everyone left behind would be guilty of the Destruction, not directly. But many. And creatures who would willingly extinguish their own species and remain so callous about all the others were the most dangerous sort. They had been taught that only the purest—only the truly innocent— could be spared. Rafeen wondered about the rightness of this too, but he obeyed the Ancients, and he accepted the limited capacity of the ship.

"The regret I hear in your voice," Nakia pressed. "Is that for the war they bring on themselves, or the loss of something so lovely?"

"Both."

Nakia exhaled angrily and pulled away from him. "They're fools."

"Yes. And yet. . . ."

Wars were not unheard of among the less developed species, but they were still mind-boggling to the more advanced races, like the Deenans. They had recorded wars on no fewer than twenty of the minor planets, where the more highly evolved beings (respectively speaking) rose up to slaughter the others. This generally happened on a smaller scale, however. Small populations might be eradicated, but rarely did the inhabitants wipe out their own existence and clear their planet to its very simplest forms of life. In fact, this would be only the second time such a thing would occur, so far as the Deenans knew. This view of the Vivid Planet would likely be obscured for millennia by whirls of noxious clouds hiding whatever still remained beneath. Only the most basic life forms would live to Resurrect the planet. Were those the true innocents?

"They're bringing it on themselves. They're doing it to *themselves*!" Nakia was fighting to hold on to her anger, twitching and shaking now with the strain of it. She wished they could save everyone, but it was impossible, and Rafeen knew it was better for Nakia to harden her heart and place blame. It would be easier for her to leave them to their Destruction that way.

"We'll save all the ones we can," he reassured her, and Nakia turned back to him and buried her face into his cool, smooth neck.

Still the ship approached the Vivid Planet.

* * * * *

Far below on the blue-green marble, a thoroughly freckled girl dragged a rusty wagon down the sidewalk. Tepid lemonade sloshed with the rumble of the wheels. Watching her, a woman sat on the stoop of her home, the door behind her hanging drunkenly from its hinges. She was hot and unhappy, and hopeless. A paper-thin T-shirt drooped from her peeling shoulders.

"Lemonade?" the girl asked. "Fifty cents."

"I'll give you a quarter."

The girl paused, considering. "You can have it free."

The woman found the drink bitter; it showed on her face. A lanky mongrel ambled up to them, tail wagging. A dirty tennis ball dropped onto one of the woman's feet, leaving a smear of dog slobber shining on her toes.

"Yuck, I don't want that!"

She pitched the ball into the neighbor's yard, beyond the chain link fence separating their trailers. The dog, who had been able to leap the fence years ago, watched it with dismay. The tail ceased its wagging, and she nosed the woman, who pushed her away.

"Get out of here!" She aimed a kick at the dog, but it didn't connect. The dog wandered over to a puddle of fetid water edged with slimy green.

The girl, feeling as sorry for the dog as she did for the woman, caressed the animal, crooning softly, and was rewarded with a friendly damp nose to the neck. The dog, even in her thirst, had never begrudged the girl a kindness.

The dog was still lapping, and the girl was still patting, when an unearthly whine sounded above them. The dog cocked her head and her tail began to raise a cloud in the dust. The girl gaped, and the woman cursed in disbelief.

* * * * *

On the other side of the world a boy is in deadly trouble.

When President-Leader Gueye found his pet rabbit, Honor, missing, he knew exactly who had done it—the grinning little miscreant with the crooked nose. He had always found the boy too fawning, too eager-to-please. Pulling back the covers in the morning from the President-Leader's silk-clothed body, setting out the President-Leader's breakfast tray in the morning, he was always grinning, nodding, bowing. And there was no one else who could have taken Honor from her cage—from Gueyer's own bedroom.

It's terribly convenient, really. President-Leader knows the boy's family sympathizes with the rebels. *Distant* family, he was told, but it's enough. Gueyer remembered the minister who convinced him to take the boy in. He will be questioned—with his family.

Before an hour has passed, Gueyer has them all rounded up. Everyone suspected of disloyalty is marched to the palace grounds. The accusations no longer matter, and if the coming executions incited the rebels, and flushed out the unfaithful members of his council, all the better. He was prepared.

The boy was not grinning now; he was quaking, visibly shaking.

"I am so sorry," Sibi said in a whisper. He had longed for the rabbit for months. She was soft and calm, and every time he held her, Sibi felt peaceful. "I have brought her back. Please!" He rushed forward and placed a cage at President-Leader's feet. Sibi knows it's foolish now, that having Honor back will change nothing. But he opens the cage door, and his face goes blank with horror.

The rabbit is gone.

"I promise," the boy cries. "She was here!"

Frantic, Sibi runs in a circle, looking vainly for the rabbit, while groans and cries arise around him in the courtyard—pleas for mercy even as President-Leader gives his order.

It is so very simple, this spark that ignites the conflagration, and President-Leader basks in the rising flames.

* * * * *

High above, in a ship that few see, enormous holds are filled with the new arrivals.

Rafeen is trying to catch Honor who is lippity-lippitying her way around the room. Animals of every sort: mice, slugs, turtles—even a whale—have a sanctuary here. A cockatoo, her flight feathers just long enough to lift her into the air, flaps down onto Rafeen's scaly head, and he bends an antenna toward her and strokes the soft contour of her neck.

There are others, of course there are, two-legged and frightened—and dangerous. They're in another area of the ship where they are being tended to separately, for their own safety, and the safety of the crew. They are young; it will be easier for them to adjust to their new lives than for their older counterparts. Still it will be harder for them than for the other animals. Some of them will never manage it.

In one of the largest holds, Nakia is greeting still more newcomers. She rolls around on the floor, her six furry legs pawing and swatting the creatures who scamper and frisk about with her. She pauses to throw balls, four-at-a-go, and puppies tear after them, exploding like shot pellets from a shell.

A few—the older dogs, with their muzzles graying, who are not able to fetch as quickly, and who have a longer memory—peer out the window to get one last glimpse of their former home below.

Key Lime Pie at the Nightmare Diner

As is the way of dreams, Amani wasn't quite sure how he had come to the little diner. He had no recollection of rolling through the door or pulling his wheelchair up to the booth, yet here he was. The smell was familiar though, the pungency of griddle grease and charcoal scent of old coffee. And the waitress seemed to recognize him.

She tucked her order pad into the pocket of her apron as she approached. She wore a warm expression and a pink nametag that read "Carlita."

"Your usual, Amani?" she asked.

"Key lime pie, black coffee, and a Coke?" Amani didn't care for coffee, but the order slid off his tongue as if on reflex.

The waitress grinned. "You're nothing if not consistent," she said. "I'll be right back."

Apart from him the diner was empty, and beyond the windows lay nothing but an abandoned parking lot illuminated by a flickering street light that kept the pitch black night at bay. Vinyl-covered swivel stools lined the short order counter, and vague kitchen sounds came from beyond the swinging doors. *Needs music*, he told himself.

At once, a jukebox he hadn't noticed before lit up and began playing "Sherri" by the Four Seasons.

Amani half-chuckled. *Love this song,* he thought. *Gotta play oldies on a jukebox.*

From the corner of his eye, Amani noticed something move beyond the window. There was a black shadow slinking, lurking through the scene framed by the window, dark on dark.

"There you go," Carlita said cheerily, settling the coffee on the table. "Don't you ever get tired of that song?"

"Do I play it a lot?"

"Every time you come in."

"How often do I come in?"

"Every night."

"Really?" He took a long pull from the straw in the glass Coke bottle and sighed. *Must be a Mexican Coke,* he thought. *That's real sugar in there, not corn syrup.*

And why shouldn't it be? It was his dream.

At that moment, the door swung open and a blast of cold air raced through the diner, ruffling napkins in their holders. A bulky figure in a fur-lined coat staggered through the door, accompanied by a flurry of snowflakes. He hurried toward Amani's booth and tipped back his hood. His raw, red hand reached out for the still steaming coffee.

"Thank you," he said, in an accent Amani couldn't place. "Didn't think I'd make it tonight. "It's blowing like a sumngun."

Amani looked out the window and saw nothing beyond the dry, empty lot. No snow out there.

At the same moment, a familiar ding echoed through the room, and Amani turned to see an elevator open where he might have expected to see a restroom door.

The straw fell from between his lips as the passengers entered the room. The first was a woman in a grey robe with full cheeks and eyebrows like crows wings. She was young, younger than Carlita, and bald. Amani scarcely had time to consider this because scampering along beside was the largest and ugliest rat Amani had ever seen. As startled as he was watching the animal traipse across the floor, it didn't compare to his shock when it hopped onto a bench and gave him a sneer.

"*Still* a possum, you idiot," it said, sharp, yellow teeth showing as he spoke. "Seriously, what's wrong with you that you can't remember from night to night?"

Amani shook his head, gaping. "Sorry."

The man flicked the possum's ear and the animal squealed and spun on him, hissing.

"Let boy alone, Chaz," said the man. "Let's just do why we are here." He caught Amani's eyes as he scooted into the booth. "I'm Neek," said the man. *Nick,* Amani corrected in his head. "Lan," he continued, gesturing palm-up to the woman, "and Chaz" he said, dropping a dark look on the possum.

"I'm dreaming," Amani said to himself.

"Genius," muttered Chaz. "You're good, kid."

Amani managed to ignore this. "But, you're all real, aren't you?"

"Of course. We're dreaming too," said Lan.

The possum rolled his ugly, beady eyes. "Again? We do this every night," he huffed.

"Then why are you here?" Amani snapped. "You're supposed to be nocturnal, aren't you? Shouldn't you be awake if we're asleep?"

Amani felt a certain satisfaction, seeing the possum taken aback. That, apparently, wasn't a question he'd asked before.

"Shaddyap and eat your pie."

"It's a tender subject," said the woman. "And we don't often talk about our waking lives here. But do eat, Amani, you'll feel better, and we can get on with our task." Everyone was looking at him now, and Amani forked a bite of the pale green pie into his mouth.

Good, he thought vaguely. *Good pie.*

The kitchen doors swung open, and Carlita swept back into the room waving menus. "Hail, hail, the gang's all here!" she sang.

"Very good," said Chaz, "What's on the menu for tonight?"

Lan flipped her menu open. "Trying to escape from danger," she read aloud. "Running through confusing building."

"Boooooring," jeered the possum.

"Looking for something in jungle. Snakes in the trees."

"No," said Nick. "No snakes."

Amani followed along on his own menu as Lan read through.

"Can't find classroom before major test. Doors keep changing."

"Locked in car sinking in ocean. Miley Cyrus singing in passenger's seat."

The next one disappeared from the menu, right before his eyes, as she read it off.

"Airplane shrinking during flight. Flying inside Kleenex box," Lan said. "Ooops, too slow. Scratch that one."

Everything was growing clearer now, and Amani felt a switch flip in his brain.

"What about this one?" he said, tapping his menu. "Losing clothing in the middle of extravagant party." That one didn't sound too hard, but the fact that a dream so banal could have life-changing consequences (and was therefore on the menu) intrigued Amani.

Nick shrugged. "Why not. You have not picked in while."

"We should be able to manage that without too much trouble," Lan said. "It's a little tame, though. We might be of better use in the Miley Cyrus one."

"The sinking car one," Amani amended.

"Nmm," said Lan. "Scary either way. Chaz?"

The possum rolled his eyes.

"We did yours last night," Amani reminded him.

"I didn't say anything, did I?" Chaz groused.

Nick clapped his hands together. "Party it is," he said, rising.

Amani wheeled himself away from the booth and started to spin himself around. Then, he remembered.

"Oh, *right!*" He removed his feet from the footrests of his wheelchair, placed them on the floor and stood up as if it were something he did any time he felt like it. The moment of surprise still struck him, though, and his legs trembled and gave way. He reached back for the arm rest, but he'd forgotten to set the brake on the chair, and it rolled out from under his hand. Amani felt himself falling, but Nick seized him by one elbow and Lan by the other.

"You've got to be convinced," said Lan.

"I'm dreaming," Amani said weakly.

Lan narrowed her eyes and squeezed his elbow. "Really convinced."

"I'm dreaming," he said again, and this time he felt the strength surge back into his legs, and he stood easily.

Nick gave a grunt of approval. "Let's go, then. Burning moonlight."

On sure footing now, Amani followed Lan, Nick, and Chaz the possum through the Men's Room door and into the nightmare.

* * * * *

It was always disorienting to enter someone else's dream. Amani sometimes found himself in a scene that resembled a half-finished basement or a preliminary sketch on a canvas that filled in as the Dreamer dreamt, but this was already pretty good.

He was in a large ballroom. Shimmering swags of purple, gold, and green swept down from the ceiling. There were pillars of balloons in the same colors, and the large, feathered half-masks of Mardi Gras stood propped around the room.

Amani blinked his eyes clear as people started to materialize.

"Oh boy. Prom." Amani hadn't been to a prom yet, and he spent the least amount of time possible dwelling on the idea. His view was suddenly blocked when he found himself surrounded by some sort of stereo equipment and a computer set-up, much of it draped with beads. "And, I'm the DJ," he muttered. "Double oh-boy." He listened for a moment to the nondescript rock song droning from the speakers. It was probably in English, but dream sounds were rarely well developed enough to be actual songs. He tapped one of the blank computer keys and the screen blared to life. Amani was trying to make sense of the play list when a bug darted across. It was the size of his thumb with glowing red eyes and a dozen legs or more. Amani recoiled with a hiss.

Dang it!

If the Tiks were already here, it was going to be a doozy of a nightmare. Amani scanned the room for the rest of the team, looking to warn them. He thought he saw Nick passing through the crowd. He was dressed in a typical marry-and-bury suit, like a high school shop teacher pressed into chaperoning the big night. Amani waved and jumped but couldn't catch his attention.

Suddenly there was a gasp in the room, and every head turned toward a couple strolling in. The girl was lovely in a shimmering purple dress that draped off her shoulders. Her curly, red hair shone like a new penny in the light. And she looked miserable. The boy beside her grimaced in an ill-fitting powder-blue tuxedo. He was well built, blonde with a strong jaw and a carriage that was somehow elegant in spite of his obvious discomfort.

He turned to his date and whispered something at her. Amani thought he was apologizing.

Which one was the Dreamer? he wondered. He became aware of a faint crackling sound, the sound made by hundreds of Tiks scurrying behind the veil of the dream.

Absently, he picked up the cup of punch that had appeared on the speaker beside him, and took a sip. It did little to alleviate the slimy metallic taste he always got when dreams started to go bad.

The newly-arrived couple made their way through the crowd as time wavered and some of the decorations disappeared to be replaced by others, shifting as the Dreamer lost track of place.

Amani was trying to keep an eye on them when a faceless girl handed him a piece of paper. He squinted down at the words. When the last of the song died, he flicked on the microphone, taking up his role.

"Ladies and gentlemen," he said into the microphone. "It's time to announce tonight's Prom royalty." Amani knew enough to know that royalty was usually preceded by attendants, but dreams never followed any rules, and the less he imposed directly in guiding the dream, the better the Tiks could be held at bay.

"Your Prom King," he announced to the eager crowd, "is Ryan Seely!"

There was a horrified gasp and murmur as the spotlight swiveled and landed on the blue-suited boy who tried to duck away from the enormous eye.

Ryan, for so he must have been, clearly hadn't expected this. He looked like a sleepwalker as he made his way to the front of the room. There was muted applause as he knelt, and a little girl slipped a sash over his shoulders and a crown on his head.

He righted himself, struggling for dignity in the face of such muted enthusiasm, and as he did a wave of hysteria broke over the room. People clapped and whooped, rocking with mirth. Ryan was completely bewildered, then he pulled the sash from his chest and looked down at the words. Upright or upside down, it wouldn't be hard to understand them—even in a dream, where reading is hard.

"Gay! Gay! Gay!" it read.

"Oh, jeez," groaned Amani. "Not that."

Ryan dropped the sash, mouth open in horror. He snatched at his head, and instead of coming up with a crown, he seized a glittering pink tiara. The sash itself had now become a sparkling white boa.

"No," he croaked, shaking his head. "It's not like that." He was on the verge of tears as the laughter rose to a shrieking pitch. His audience pointed and clutched at their faces. Some were chanting now. "Gay! Gay! Gay!"

Ryan shook, humiliated. His blue suit disappeared and was immediately replaced with a glittering golden speedo swim suit and nothing more. He tried to cover himself with his hands and skitter away, but his legs were as useless as Amani's in his chair. Amani had seen that "Nightmare Freeze" before, and he launched into action.

"What to do?" he breathed, scanning his tools. The best way to enrage the Tiks was to engage directly with the Dreamer. But if you could change the scene in your own role, that was the wisest approach.

"Be a D.J. then," he said to himself. Amani turned to his computer, scrolled through the songs on the screen and clicked.

That same second, a swell of music filled the room and the lights went out. A spotlight poured down on the middle of the room, illuminating a bald Britney Spears singing along with "Nothing Compares 2 U."

It was Lan, of course, in a rusty orange sheath dress that made Amani do a double-take. But he could also see just how Ryan's dream brain was interpreting it. Dreamily-mistaken with his singers, but not unreasonable, as both Britney and Sinead O'Connor had been bald at one time or another.

"Atta woman!" he thought. He was so taken with Lan's performance, that he nearly forgot about his Dreamer, and Amani spun back to see Ryan taking advantage of the audience's distraction to finally flee. He was wrapping something around his waist and stumbling away from the stage.

The dream was shifting now. One of the balloon pillars had become some sort of doorway in Ryan's mind. Amani's stomach was roiling, but he quickly followed Ryan through.

This time he couldn't see anything but a steamy blur; fortunately there were other clues. He was panting with nerves, almost smothering in the humid air. The smell of chlorine clung in the air, and a prairie of hot concrete warmed the soles of his feet.

Ah, a swimming pool, he realized. *Ryan was wrapping a towel around himself.* And the image quickly assembled itself before his eyes.

Amani found himself pacing the pool deck, a red buoy under his arm. He spied Nick at a busy concession stand. He didn't have a bead on Lan yet, nor Chaz who often found it more difficult to slip himself unnoticed into dreams.

And where was Ryan?

There! In the 12-foot end. He was swimming along next to the wall.

Amani walked slowly, pretending to keep watch over the placeholder swimmers populating the dream, and all the while moving toward Ryan.

He couldn't see any Tiks yet but the crawling feeling was inside of him. He hadn't felt so sick in a dream in a very long time. The moment he saw the sash, Amani had regretted making the Nightmare selection. He tried to breathe, focusing on the freckles of sunlight reflected off the water. Then, he saw it. A black patch. Then another. The water was growing dark and thick with swimming Tiks.

Amani's fingers were numb and he dropped the whistle as he tried to raise it to his lips.

This was going to go badly either way; Amani didn't think he could wait for Ryan to make first contact. Fortunately, Ryan saw his situation a split second later. The whites shone around Ryan's eyes as he called for help.

"Grab on!" Amani screamed. He flung the buoy and pulled it into position, but Tiks had already swarmed Ryan. Ryan grabbed the buoy with one arm and tried to paddle through the bug-riddled water with his free arm. His chin was raised, and his lips were pulled back in a silent scream.

"Shut your mouth! Close your mouth!" Amani hollered, but Ryan was deafened by his fear. To Amani's horror one dark Tik scrabbled up his chin and disappeared into his mouth.

Damn it! Damn it! He nearly threw down the line in disgust.

The rest of the Tiks disappeared then, their job done, and Ryan scrambled out onto the pool deck, dripping and panting.

"It's a nightmare!" he said to Amani as he tried to gain his feet. "This can't be real. I have to wake up!"

Amani grabbed his arm. "Ryan. You're right, it is a nightmare," he said quickly. "But you need to stick with it. We need to ride it through and work it out now, if you don't want it to follow you."

"Follow me?" He jerked his arm from Amani's grip. "The nightmare?" He looked back into the pool, where the water was now clear and empty, and his eyes glazed.

"That bug that just went inside of you? That's called a Tik. You'll carry it out of the dream with you if you don't deal with it now."

"Are you part of the dream?" he asked.

Oh, but he was sharp! Amani was oddly proud of being in Ryan's dream. Most Dreamers could scarcely link one thought to the next.

"I'm a…visitor," he explained. "Look, we don't have time to talk about this right now, but you have to make a decision to stay or that Tik is going to be with you when you're awake. It's going to ruin you. But, you can get rid of it if you face your nightmare. It's what nightmares are for, man. They're a trial run."

Ryan's breathing had slowed. "What do I have to do?"

"You have to go back."

"Back? Back to the dance?" He looked over his shoulder back to the locker rooms and pinched his eyes shut. "If it's just a dream, why is it so hard?" he asked.

"Because it's your fear. Nightmare or not."

"I'm scared. I'm a coward," Ryan said.

"Being scared doesn't mean you're a coward," Amani argued. "If you're never afraid, you can never be brave. To be brave is to face fear."

Ryan considered this for a moment then looked directly into Amani's eyes.

"Have *you*?" Ryan asked him. "Have *you* faced the fear?"

The question hit him in the sternum and sent a shockwaves along his rib. "I-I can't talk about that here," Amani stammered. It was mostly true, but he would have evaded the question even if it weren't. "But I can tell you that facing your fear here will help you face it out there."

Ryan shook his head, fighting the nightmare scenarios in his head.

"You won't be alone," said Amani. "I'm here to help you, and so are my friends."

"If I do this now, it will be easier... later?"

Amani swallowed down the bitter taste of his hypocrisy. "Absolutely."

Amani wasn't sure he'd convinced him; there was a long pause as Ryan closed his eyes and searched for something inside of himself. When he opened his eyes, though, he gave a noisy exhale, set his shoulders, and started back toward the locker rooms.

* * * * *

The dance was again in full swing, but this time Ryan was a man on a mission. From his position in the sound equipment, Amani watched him extend an arm to Lan.

"*Oye Como Va*," he mouthed to Amani, who obliged by clicking the song to life on the computer.

Well, I should have expected that, Amani thought as Ryan spun Lan into his arms. He had seen that dancer's posture when Ryan had first entered the room. The other dancers shuffled aside, creating a ring of rapt spectators around them. Lan was beaming, and Ryan all snap and polish as they cha-chaed across the floor.

The "Gay!" sash appeared in Ryan's hand then, for he'd conjured it, and he ducked into it in one quick move, while he spun Lan with the other arm.

People were staring, amazed. They were watching a dancer. A whoop rose from the crowd and a responding cheer as the couple lit up the floor. Over the noise of the crowd and the flash of the spectacle, Amani never noticed the yellow swag above billowing dangerously toward the floor, sagging.

Nick, the dance chaperone, burst onto the scene.

"Everybody, move back!" He yelled, waving people away from the floor.

Ryan stumbled backward with Lan, and everyone looked up at the bulging swag. It was swelling like a balloon, and Amani had to duck past it to get to Ryan's side. He heard Lan tell him, "Get ready."

"That's more than enough," said a sneering voice. A white streak shot through the air. It was Chaz, lunging toward the swelling mass. He ripped a line down the swag and Tiks poured from the gash.

The air was filled with screams and fleeing bodies in shimmering dresses and sharp suits.

"Fight!" screamed Amani. "We have to fight them!" He was already stomping and his teeth clacked against one another. Ryan never hesitated, and Lan pushed over one of the mask props and began jumping on it, and over the screams Amani thought he could hear the crackle of a thousand dying Tiks.

More Tiks rained from the ceiling. Chaz was covered with them, fighting and spinning and hissing.

"They're still coming!" Ryan screamed. "I have to wake up!"

"No! Don't!" Amani flinched as a blast of air slashed past him, and he turned to see a scruffy Prom goer swinging at the mass of Tiks with a folded chair.

The scruffy boy gave Ryan a thumbs-up before swinging at the Tiks again. "We're for you, Dude." Several hundred Tiks were blown away by the strength of the next blast.

"Proud of you!" said a girl, swinging with another chair.

One girl was pounding Tiks left and right with the fancy street shoes she'd worn under her dress. "Honestly? I always kind of thought you might be, Ryan." She gave him a wink and never slowed her Tik bashing.

Their encouragement gave Ryan a second wind and he pushed over a table, crushing yet more Tiks beneath. It looked like they would hold their own against the Dream beasts, when another black bulge swelled down from the ceiling. Not a swag, but an enormous Tik, round and fat as a Macy's Parade float, landed in the middle of the room.

Amani's stomach turned to ice. All of the fight left him, and he tripped, sliding on the slime of Tik bodies. But Ryan was fire-eyed now. Nothing was going to stop him.

He jerked a large cardboard tube away from a mask decoration and ran for the Tik's vulnerable belly, bellowing as he went. A moment later, the cardboard tube transformed into an enormous sword and disappeared into the beast.

The Tik jerked and roared as Ryan drove it through. Ryan heaved and tore the Tik's belly open. Insides spilled over the floor. String upon string of Mardi Gras beads gushed from the wound. They bounced and rolled in a kaleidoscope of color. Every Tik and Tik carcass became a sequin or rhinestone, and the floor was awash with color and shimmer.

Ryan dropped the sword and fell to his knees as he watched the crowd cheer and dive for the baubles.

Amani gradually found his feet, and made his shaking way toward Ryan. He was vaguely aware of Chaz on the refreshments table, eating cookies. On the other side of the room Lan was draping a fistful of green beads around Nick's neck, a gesture he accepted with a grimace.

"Ready to go?" Amani asked.

Ryan had a black tuxedo on now, and a legitimate crown on his head, but he didn't appear to notice at all.

"Yeah. I guess I am."

* * * * *

"Seriously, order some pie," said Amani. "It'll make you feel better."

Ryan picked up the unused coffee spoon and scooped a piece of Amani's half-eaten Key lime from earlier in the night.

"Or, you're welcome to that one," Amani continued. "No, seriously, it's fine," he said when Ryan cut him a look. Amani wasn't hungry at all, he didn't think his stomach could handle it anyway.

They had all returned to the diner. Sometimes after a traumatic dream, it was better to take a Dreamer there to debrief. This was one of those nights.

Ryan tapped the spoon in the air, gathering his thoughts. "Who were those other people helping us? They weren't part of your. . . team?" he said, looking around the table from Lan to Nick to Amani and Chaz.

"No. Only us," said Nick.

"There are other people who will support you though," said Lan. "In your heart, you must know that because they showed up in your dream. You have to trust that."

Ryan nodded and took another bite of pie.

Across the table Amani sipped his now-flat Coke and tried to ignore a niggling itch on his back. He hadn't been able to find it, and it was driving him crazy.

Chaz, who was seated on the bench beside Amani, reached up and placed his front paws on the table. His whiskers whirred, and he fixed his eyes on Ryan who twitched under his beady stare.

"So, here's my question," he began, his voice like a sneer. "Why do you need support? Why don't you just keep it to yourself? Or, just not be gay?" He gave an animal cough. "You danced with two girls tonight, right? Why don't you just keep doing that?"

Ryan's mouth popped open, but nothing came out.

"Chaz," Nick groaned.

Amani rubbed his lips together trying to fight back a retort. Chaz was a possum. He couldn't be expected to understand anything. But Amani also remembered Ryan's bravery that night, and couldn't let Chaz go on unchallenged. "You can't stop being gay," he said. "Just like you can't stop being a possum."

"How would *you* know?" Chaz snapped.

"Just like you can't stop being a jerk," Amani continued, voice raised.

Chaz barked a high mocking laugh. "Fat lot you know, kid."

Amani's blood boiled now. He wanted to grab that little furry throat and squeeze, but instead he let his anger fuel his courage.

"I do know," he said. "I know because...because I'm gay too. I just am." It was a relief in dozen different ways. Amani had never said it aloud before. Not here. Not anywhere.

But wasn't that what a dream was for? A trial run?

The itch behind his neck was unbearable now. He slapped at it, and the sensation raced down his arm. A Tik darted out from his sleeve then and made a wild leap for the floor.

"Geez!" Amani yelped, flapping out his arm. "I didn't realize I had one!"

Lan gave a sharp cry of surprise, and Chaz leapt from the table and snapped up the Tik with a crunch.

"That wasn't so hard was it?" the possum said, looking smug. Amani shuddered as Chaz smacked and licked his teeth clean. "Gotcha, kid. Don't say I never did nothing for ya." He gave a flick of his tail and slipped out the cat door that had appeared in the wall.

* * * * *

"You'll forget most of this." Amani told Ryan after Nick and Lan had gone. "You'll remember the Prom and how you felt, but you won't remember the swimming pool or the Tiks. Your mind will do something different with them."

Ryan nodded soberly. "Will we see each other again, do you think?"

"Do you often have recurring dreams?"

"I don't think so. But, I mean in real life?"

Amani sighed. "I live in   "

Ryan's eyebrows crinkled. "What? I didn't get that."

"You can text me at   " Amani said.

"Ahh, I see," replied Ryan. "We can't exchange that sort of information here can we?"

Amani was still impressed at how quickly Ryan could pick things up. It was hard for a Dreamer to be so lucid, even in the diner. It made the reality that much more bitter.

"Yep," he said. "There's no way to share contact information in a dream. We can't speak it aloud, and if we were to try to write it the pencil wouldn't work. I don't know what would happen if we tried sign language. I sort of don't want to risk it," he added, wriggling his fingers once on the table top. "It seems unfair. You won't remember being in the diner at all anyway. And if we've done a good job, you won't come back here either."

"Oh, and you can leave any time you like," Amani added, nodding toward a new door in the wall, one that likely led to Ryan's bedroom.

"What about you?" Ryan asked. "Are you stuck here until I leave?"

"Nah, we can leave at any time. Lan and Nick like to leave early, so they'll come in clear-headed the next night. I stay as late as I can, until Carlita kicks me out, at least" he said, with a chuckle. "So, when I come back each night, I'm confused at first. It always takes me a while to remember what I'm doing here, like I'm a Dreamer too."

"Why do you stay late?"

Amani nodded to his wheelchair which was tucked in at the adjoining booth. "That's mine."

Ryan blinked. "Oh," he said. "In real life."

"Yep. But I can do anything here—run, jump. Walk. It's part of my dream."

Ryan was quiet for a moment, and Amani wondered if he'd made a mistake telling Ryan of his handicap. Sometimes people changed when they learned something new about you. Sometimes they were frightened, but the friends and the people who really cared didn't. He needed to remember that.

He was trying to think of something to say, when Ryan jumped up from the table.

"Huh, a jukebox," he said, clearly delighted. "I have only seen a jukebox like once in my life!" He scanned the list of songs and turned toward Amani with an excited smile. "Can you. . .do you dance?"

"I do *here*. I'm not any good, but I try." He lifted a shoulder and let it drop.

"I do ballroom," Ryan said.

"I figured. I saw your moves."

"Oh yeah." Ryan grinned, recalling. "This is an amazing song list," he said.

"There's anything you want on there," said Amani.

Ryan gave another "huh," and tapped in his selection. Bob Marley's "Three Little Birds" played from some unseen speakers overhead.

Ryan offered Amani a hand up from the booth.

"I'll show you how to two-step. It's not too hard."

"I really don't think I'll be any good."

"Who'll know?" Ryan asked lightly.

Amani felt his cheeks warm with pleasure, and one little bird seemed to flitter in his own stomach as he stood. "So, show me then."

And though neither of them would ever remember it, Amani and Ryan danced happily till dawn, fueled on hope and Key lime pie in the Nightmare Diner.

god-thing

It was the most gawd-awful-stupid "art" Sadie'd ever seen; only a supernatural injustice could explain the blue ribbon attached to it. The entry card propped next to it on the table read *Buckshot High School,* "god-thing," *First Place in Sculpture.* She huffed a dry laugh and shook her head.

The boy beside her regarded the sculpture with equal disgust. In his hand, he clutched a small, green vase. It was round as a perfect gourd and green as an emerald. And ribbon-less.

"What *is* that? 'god-thing?'" he said with a sneer. "I don't get it."

Sadie shrugged. "Well, the way I understand it—it's a Styrofoam ball with plastic googley-eyes all over. That could represent the all-seeing aspect of God. It sees in all directions and the eyes never close." The boy squinted at her, so Sadie continued. "The sequins and heart-shaped rhinestones are to make it beautiful, and so people will love it. And the feathers are soft to touch, and they make you feel good. People like gods because of the way they make them feel," Sadie explained.

The boy shook his head. "It's just dumb. And it's fugly as hell!" he protested.

"I agree."

"I wonder who made it."

Sadie grinned wickedly. "I did."

* * * * *

Sadie had moved to Buckshot, Mississippi ("Drive straight toward Hell. You'll get there.") three months before the end of the school year. As a free-thinking Northerner, she struggled to adjust to the land of Right-wingers, "Funda-gelicals" and Creationism in science class. Sadie had found herself almost completely at-odds with the prevailing school culture. Unaccountably, her closest friend, Martha, was a sharp-tongued Baptist with five younger brothers and sisters.

Martha asked Sadie about the "inspiration" behind her work with a thoughtful expression.

"You know how everyone says, 'It's a God-thing' when something really good happens?" Sadie began. "Like, 'I was totally hung-over, but I still aced my chemistry test. It must have been a God-thing!' 'I just totally found my keys in the refrigerator before I was late! What a God-thing!' Or, 'I was driving with my headlights off and almost hit a bicyclist. It was a total God-thing that I missed her!' The God-thing is always saving the day." *For idiots*, she added in her head.

Martha nodded. "I see what you mean."

Sadie was surprised that the art show judges had been so open-minded and had awarded anything to her piece—she had meant it as a joke, or a social commentary, maybe—but perhaps they didn't get it. As for the rest of her schoolmates, Sadie couldn't resist rubbing it in a little.

Instead of taking her sculpture home for the last three weeks of school, Sadie re-arranged her locker to create a small shrine for her. ("Yes, *of course* the god-thing's female!")

Derek, whose locker boasted bumper stickers reading "Real Men Love Jesus" and "Don't Just Stand There, Pray Something!" watched as Sadie made a show of stroking the feathers of her god-thing.

"What are you doing?" he asked.

Deliberately, Sadie placed a blue M&M in front of the god-thing before shutting the locker door.

"Just asking for extra help on my algebra final. Mr. Haus said I did great on my Spanish final, and I figure it was the god-thing."

"You really think it helps you?"

"As much as your deity helps you," Sadie said.

"But God is real."

"So is the god-thing. See?" She opened the locker again to offer proof, but Derek just rolled his eyes.

Sadie told herself not to be disappointed; superstition ran strong among her classmates. They had been trained by their culture and families, and each Sunday their houses of worship were filled with people insisting that their myth of choice was the only certainty.

She felt bad for them.

Sadie's algebra final went brilliantly, and she left another M&M for the god-thing before her physics final. Just for laughs.

* * * * *

"Are you going to display it in your house?" Martha asked on the last day of school.

"This ugly thing?" Martha's grin of acknowledgment reflected Sadie's. "If it were a little smaller, I'd hang it from my rearview mirror as a totem or something, but I think I'll just put it on my dresser."

Turned out, putting it on her dresser was a mistake. That night, Sadie awoke to moonlight glinting off a dozen unblinking eyes. The god-thing was not colorful now; darkness made it into something that might have clung to a crumbling cathedral or abandoned cemetery. It was a gargoyle, lurking in the corner of her room, leering at her while she slept. Sadie turned over to avoid looking at it, but she did not like having the thing at her back. Prickles ran down her spine, and gooseflesh pricked her arms. Eventually Sadie got up, placed the god-thing in the closet, and shut the door.

It was a warm night, but she pulled the covers over herself anyway and wiped her hand across the sheet to remove the feeling of the god-thing from her palm.

* * * * *

By morning, Sadie thought no more of it. The sequins glinted silver and blue and orange, and Sadie gave it a finger-tip pat as she rummaged for sandals in her closet.

Summer was the transition from school to softball, but even that was tainted with religion. Martha led the team's pre-game prayer and, after losing their first three games, the shortstop made team bracelets using softball shaped beads with a Christian cross bead at the latch. Sadie felt obliged to wear it, but since the bracelet flew off every time she batted, Sadie offered hers to the god-thing. She closed the clasp and draped it over top of her faux-icon where it dangled bisecting several plastic eyes. That's when the winning streak began. Sadie laughed at the coincidence but gave the god-thing a Hershey's Kiss when her team went to the summer league championship. She ate that same kiss when they lost to the Midland Rangers two weeks later.

But that's not really superstition, Sadie told herself, it was a silly ritual that helped her laugh at people who took such things seriously. It was no different than Martha's pre-game prayer in that it didn't really do anything. And she wasn't foisting her ritual on anyone else. So, why shouldn't she enjoy it?

* * * * *

"We're hosting a barbecue for our church youth group tonight, and Mom and Papa said you're invited. It won't be a big Jesus-push—" Martha added quickly, savvy enough to anticipate the objection. "It's just a get-together."

Sadie considered this. She had gone to Victory Baptist Church exactly one time and sworn it off after a hell-fire sermon. It had been an awkward experience, and she had no desire to relieve it in any form—but she adored Martha's family. Sadie had no siblings of her own, and she loved the attention of Martha's rambunctious brothers and sisters.

Then her thoughts swung to one other person. Thane Peterson. He attended Martha's church, where she'd originally met him, but went to another high school, and their paths rarely crossed. She drummed her fingers along her leg as she remembered. He was tall and lean, with a certain hard-to-identify ease in his manner. He played basketball and trumpet. And if he knew he was good looking, he wasn't hung-up on it. He had a confidence that, instead of making everyone feel intimidated, elevated them as well.

Sadie realized she was smiling as she thought of him, but she would be damned (so to speak) if she'd ask whether Thane would actually be there.

"Yeah, I'll come. Thanks for the invite."

Sadie hung up, telling herself that spending the evening with Martha's family would be worth it either way.

Grabbing a shirt from the closet, she patted the god-thing on the head. The black eyes clicked. "Wish me luck! . . . And make me pretty and clever. And make Thane clever enough to notice," she added in a conspiratorial whisper.

It was nearly a moot request.

The party was in full swing when Sadie arrived. She fielded a warm hug from Martha's mom, who met her at the door. "We're glad you came. Martha and the others are in the back. Get yourself a snack and we'll have burgers after a bit."

The spacious back yard was alive with chattering teens drinking soda and laughing loudly. But she had no sooner arrived at the cookie table when Martha's little sister Naomi pounced upon her, nearly snatching Sadie's hand from her arm.

"Push me, please!"

"Ok." Sadie reached out and gave the little girl a nudge on the shoulder. "How was that?"

Naomi laughed, baring all of her 5-year-old teeth. "No, on the swing!" She seized a chocolate cookie and thrust it at Sadie. "Eat this for good energy."

"Thaaaanks." She took the cookie between her fingertips. No telling where those grubby little mitts had been.

Sadie gave in with feigned reluctance and ate her cookie and pushed Naomi on the swing until the little girl was exhausted with laughing. Then she kicked around a hacky sack with a couple of the little brothers, before Martha eventually rescued her and she got to chat with her own peers for a bit.

"I'm sorry the kids are always all over you," Martha said.

"It's fine," Sadie said. And she wasn't even trying to be nice about it. It was a good evening, even if Thane wasn't coming.

Eventually smoke began drifting up from the grills and everyone began edging toward the sizzling meat.

Pastor Mike took his opportunity to say a prayer before anyone could poison themselves on unblessed food, and it was then that Sadie finally spied him. Thane. He stood across from her, looking calmly at the ground and lightly joggling his baseball cap at his side. He was the only other person with his eyes open.

Was it luck, or something more that cause the two of them to quietly catch one another's eyes among the bowed heads? Sadie gave him the faintest smile, and Thane waggled an eyebrow at her. In the next moment, Pastor Mike "Amen"-ed, and Naomi appeared again to clutch her hand.

"We gotta get us a hot dog for energy," said Naomi. The pig-tailed 5-year-old dragged Sadie to the buffet table, and away from Thane who watched them with an amused expression. Naomi kept close to Sadie's elbow as they negotiated the buffet table, just to be sure she got enough to eat and commenting on her choices all the while.

"Get another pickle," Naomi insisted. "It will make you healthy."

"It's unhealthy to get too healthy," Sadie told her, and Naomi's face twisted as she tried to make sense of this.

Fortunately, by the time darkness settled, Martha's mother had called off the youngest of her brood, and Thane had taken her place. He handed her a chocolate chip cookie by the by the light of a tiki-torch.

"Dessert?" he said. "I noticed that little girl ate all of yours."

"She just wanted me to be healthy," Sadie explained.

"I noticed you shirked the prayer, too," Thane said, and Sadie pressed her lips together, fearing for a moment that it might have been a rebuke. Then, she snorted.

"I could say the same for you. What are you doing watching me anyway?"

He winked at her, in mute admission. "I've heard about you."

"Oh, I bet."

"All good, to my way of thinking." He looked at her steadily now, with a glint in his eye, and Sadie blinked away, self-conscious. In the distance she saw Martha and two other youth group kids chasing fireflies through the trees. Thane's voice drew her back.

"Martha said you'd be here tonight," he said.

"She did?"

"Yep. I asked."

Sadie was shocked. Thane had been interested in *her*? "Oh," she croaked. "Yeah, I'm . . . definitely here."

"I can tell." Thane grinned. "Anyway, I saw you playing hacky sack. You're pretty good."

Sadie nodded and examined a potato chip. "I used to play soccer."

"Used to?"

"Got too hard on my knees," she explained.

"So, you took up softball?"

"And how do you know *that*?"

"You have a reputation. You're a spit-fire," he said on a laugh. "That's awesome." Thane grinned at her in a way that made her toes curl. After a half-hour of chatter, he knew quite a bit more about her, and Sadie had learned enough of Thane to be far more than smitten.

Sadie was practically singing in her room that night as she threw open her closet door.

"Thank you!" she trilled at the god-thing. "I should have brought you a chocolate chip."

She stopped then and considered the god-thing—and the defacto shrine—with disgust.

Am I really doing this? She asked herself. *Tonight's a high-point for my whole year—and I'm sharing it with. . . that?*

Sadie snatched the god-thing and rummaged through the kitchen drawers until she found some matches.

Out by the garage, she dropped her god-thing in a trash can, tossed in some newspaper, and struck a flame. It was a moment of dark determination when she lit her own twist of newspaper and set the rest alight. The paper went up quickly, but the god-thing didn't ignite; it deformed. The Styrofoam oozed into grey-edged slicks, the feathers stank, and the little black disks rattled as the clear globes of the eyes melted.

She hadn't thought it could grow uglier, but she'd been wrong.

That night in her bed, Sadie felt an odd sense of relief.

Funny how easily I almost got tricked into that. Believing in a stupid Styrofoam ball. Not so much stranger than an invisible person in the sky. But, I got rid of it. I did it.

She slept, feeling stronger, vindicated, and ready to move forward with empathy toward those snookered by religious faith.

The next morning, over a late breakfast of cold cereal, the phone rang. Martha's quavering voice on the other end was scarcely recognizable.

"Sadie!"

"Martha, are you ok?"

Martha swallowed audibly. "Our house burned down last night."

"Oh my god! Are you ok?" Sadie was so stunned she forgot to watch her speech. Martha either didn't notice or didn't care.

"We got out. Dad and Naomi are in the hospital from the smoke. They flew Naomi to Jackson, cause she was littler, and . . . it was worse for her. But the doctors think she'll be ok."

Sadie's heart squeezed painfully, and she leaned against the wall.

"Oh, poor baby. I'm glad she's going to be ok." She rubbed the tight place in her chest with her palm. "What can I do, Martha? I can bring you some clothes. Or. . . do you need a place for your brother and sisters to go? Do you? I can—"

"Thanks *so* much," Martha sounded on the edge of tears suddenly. "Lots of church families are already helping, though. We're headed down to Jackson today, and we've got some folks down there to help with the little ones." She sighed. "I just wanted to tell you."

"I'm glad you did, Martha. I'm so sorry! Please, if there's anything you need, *please* let me know." Sadie's mind was reeling. What could she offer? A dozen questions raced through her mind. "A fire! That's horrible! How did it start?"

Martha calmed herself, perhaps preferring to focus on the simple facts rather than the emotional strain. "They think it started by the garage," she said. "Someone might've put something in a garbage can that smoldered until nighttime. Maybe one of the matches to light the tiki torches." She sighed again, almost a groan. "Nothing's certain though."

Sadie went slowly numb, and a creeping cold spread across her skin.

No. Nothing's *certain.*

She scarcely remembered offering her final condolences before hanging up. After several long moments, Sadie forced her trembling legs to carry her outside. The garbage can shrieked with the twist of old metal as she removed the lid, and a faint smell of smoke reached her nostrils. With an effort, she reached inside . . .and found the god-thing—still warm.

Sadie jerked back her hand with a gasp and looked down. From the shadowy depth of the can, the god-thing peered back up at her with one, large unmelted eye.

The Coal Room

You always have to tell the truth to police officers. Iris knew that rule since she was a little girl. As young as her little sister Mia, even.

But she was old enough now to know that even police can't see the truth sometimes.

"Now, can you tell me again? When was the last time you saw your sister?" Officer Reeves asked. She was a short woman with a somber expression and hair dyed the color of rust. She reminded Iris of an old fire hydrant.

"She was going downstairs in our house," Iris said.

"And what did she say?"

"She said she was going to the coal room."

Officer Reaves tapped her pen on the notebook where she was writing. Wrinkles appeared between her eyebrows.

"But your parents say there is no coal room in your house. Not in the basement or anywhere. Do you think Mia might have been playing a game? Did she have a secret hideout or play place that she might think of as the coal room?"

"She said she was going to the coal room," Iris repeated helplessly.

The wind picked up, ruffling the papers of the notebook, and Iris turned her back to the blast.

Everyone was standing on the porch, Iris and Officer Reeves, Iris's Mom and Dad, and her big brother Fritz, who wrapped his arms around himself as he talked with the tall male officer. They all looked at one another as thunder shook the sky and the window panes of the old house buzzed in their sills.

"Let's go back inside," Officer Reeves said, as the rain began to pour. "We've called up some more officers to scour the grounds. We want to bring in all the people we can before it gets too dark."

Iris met eyes with her brother. Fritz was strained and anxious looking, and the cords in his neck twitched like he might start hollering Mia's name again as he had been when they first realized their little sister was truly missing.

The male officer, Officer Garcia, opened the door, and waved them inside. "We're going to go through the house room by room, okay? It's a big property, but we'll find her."

Iris's mother made a horrible sound, a sound like a sob, and Iris hunched her shoulders against it, like it was another cold gust of wind.

"We're going to find her," said her father. "I promise. We'll find her." He placed a kiss on her mother's forehead, and she looked faintly comforted by this.

But Iris, who knew something about truth, was not comforted. She knew they would not find Mia.

* * * * *

Mia first told Iris about the coal room when they were playing hide-and-seek a month after they had moved in to their new country home.

"Where were you?" Iris demanded as her sister emerged from the basement. "I've been looking for you forever!"

"I don't have to say." Mia folded her arms over her chest. "You said 'ollie ollie oxen free' means you give up, and you don't have to say where you were hiding. Plus, you were supposed to have your eyes closed anyway," she added, belatedly realizing the injustice. She was six now, and her sense of fairness was strong.

"I was all *over* the basement. I looked everywhere!" exclaimed Iris. "And how did you get so dirty? You're covered in . . . what *is* that? It's pitch black," she said, swiping a finger across her sister's arm and examining the residue on her fingertips

"It's my secret!"

"I'm gonna tell Mom if you don't fess up. You might get yourself stuck somewhere you can't get out, and she's gonna go nuts when she sees how dirty you got your clothes. Tell me!"

Mia sighed and rolled her eyes—something she had learned from Iris.

"I was in the coal room," she said.

Iris glowered. "There's no coal room downstairs." Downstairs was nothing more than a big storage area. The concrete-and-stone foundation was bare, and some walls that had once been framed out had been abandoned, like the decaying furniture left by some previous owner. And there were mice. At least Fritz said there were, but Iris hadn't found them, and she'd tried.

Also Mom and Dad said not to play down there, but they were bored.

"Ok," said Mia with a shrug. "So, I wasn't in the coal room."

"Moooom!" Iris hollered. "Mia is filthy again!"

But this time, the joke was on Iris. Their mother, who was painting the kitchen, merely groaned to see the state of her younger daughter and sent Iris to scrub her down in the bathtub.

Mia looked smug.

* * * * *

Iris followed Officer Garcia back into the basement. He tried the light switch, and the naked bulb popped, illuminating the dark bowels of the house with a brief flash before dying.

"Why don't you head back upstairs," he told Iris, pulling a flashlight from his belt. "You might trip on something down here."

"I'm ok. I'm just going to stand here," Iris said. She watched the sweep of the flashlight and the bizarre shadows it threw, passing over the old chests, the hulk of a wardrobe and even the decrepit bureau drawers, the same ones they had already been through. But Officer Garcia examined them again while Iris closed her eyes in the corner of the room and waited.

"You know, once we found a little boy hiding under a bathroom sink, in the cupboard behind the towels," Officer Garcia said, dropping a sheet back over a pile of old chairs. "He'd been there over three hours. You wouldn't think a kid could do that, especially with people calling for him, but he thought it was a pretty funny game. And with a house this big and sprawling?" The flashlight bobbed as the officer shrugged, "There are lots of good hiding places that only little kids come up with."

"It's a real fixer-upper," muttered Iris. That was what her Dad had said, glowing with pride, the day they pulled into the drive.

There was a bang and a roar of thunder that seemed to hum through the stones of the foundation. Iris reached her arms into the empty space, reached her mind, listened, and felt.

It's storming, she whispered to herself. *It's definitely storming now. So where are you?*

A warm breath of air slithered past her neck, and Iris turned in anticipation.

* * * * *

It was a dare that led Iris to the coal room for the first time.

The sky was black, the wind had been blowing all day, and Fritz's baseball game had been called for lightning. Iris was bored of duct tape designing, and the Internet was down. Desperate times called for desperate measures, and the siblings turned to one another for entertainment.

"I dare you," said Fritz, "to hold an ice cube in your mouth until it melts." Iris's teeth and tongue ached after that one, and she returned like for like.

"I dare you to do a long division problem with a crayon, holding it in your teeth." Fritz always complained that math was physically painful to him as it was, but he muddled through. Eventually.

"I dare you to go into the basement with the lights off and sit there for three minutes," he countered.

"We're not supposed to go down there," argued Iris. She didn't so much care about her parents' strictures, but she did not love the dark.

Fritz shrugged. "It's a dare. Are you going to take it or not?"

"No, pick something else."

"If you do it, you'll win," Fritz grinned, and this goaded Iris's competitive spirit. Fritz always won everything even though he was only a year older.

Three minutes, she told herself. She could suffer the dark of the basement for three minutes.

Iris set her teeth and headed toward the stairwell.

"I'm closing the door behind you," Fritz said, when Iris had reached the basement landing. "It's got to be pitch black. Ok, *now*."

The door closed and the sound echoed off the stony walls. A moment later, the slice of light that shone beneath the door was blotted out from the other side. Fritz was nothing if not thorough. Iris had never seen blackness like this before. It was so dark that it wasn't even scary. Not at first. It was as if nothing could exist in such a darkness. Not even a wicked imagination. Not even Iris.

She forced herself to breathe, though inhaling was a strain. She sang "You are My Sunshine" in her head, unwilling to make actual sound. Her voice would have shaken anyway, frightening her more. But she was going to win this—if Fritz opened the door at three minutes.

He'd better!

Time ticked past giving her time to sing two more songs, before Iris's insides began to itch with anxiety. She was about to start crawling toward the stairs when she felt a breeze on her face. She flinched and cowered, and then noticed a faint light as if through a curtain.

To her left. She saw it clearly then. A sheer curtain the full height of the wall, gray and wafting, almost like a spider's web, bellowing in a breeze. Had she ever seen this before? Iris watched as her hand reached out and moved the curtain aside to reveal a small coal room on the other side.

Whoa! Iris breathed.

The room was the size of a large closet. Above her head and to the right was a window, dingy and covered by layers of cobwebs and some sort of plant on the outside. It let in just enough light for her eyes to adjust. A pile of coal took up an entire corner of the room and spilled against the adjacent walls. There didn't seem to be a door, only the curtain still draped against her wrist.

Iris stepped inside and felt the musty air on her lips and in her nostrils. She reached out to touch one of the shining clumps of coal and admired the sooty black on her fingertips. The walls weren't like those of her basement, and one of the stones appeared to be out of place. She wiggled it, and it came away from the wall, revealing a small cache behind it. Disbelieving, Iris fingered an ancient bit of string—good for cats-cradles, maybe; a wooden top; several badly damaged glass marbles; and crude human-shaped figurines carved from coal and no bigger than her fist. She wondered how long they'd been down there. Maybe a hundred years.

How old is our house? Iris wondered.

From the gloom, Iris heard someone snicker.

"Fritz?" she hissed, peeking from behind the curtain.

Suddenly, light poured down the stairway, followed by footsteps, and the flare of the overhead light.

"Hey! I said times-up about five minutes ago," barked Fritz, when he reached the basement. "What, were you going to hide and jump out at me?"

"Come here and see this!" she said, brushing out from the coal room. Iris reached back to push the curtain aside and came up with nothing but empty space. The stone foundation lay several feet beyond her reach, and her arm hung worthless in the air.

"What?" grumped Fritz.

Iris squinted and waved her hand again through the air and came up empty.

"Never mind," she muttered.

"You shouldn't hide from people," Fritz said with a huff. "It's not funny."

* * * * *

"He's too old. That's why Fritz can't find it," Mia said.

"I can't find it all the time either," Iris said. "I mean, I never found it until today and I've been down there lots of times before."

"You're almost too old, too," her sister said, nibbling a graham cracker. "*You* can only find the coal room when there's a storm. That's what Silas says." Mia looked suddenly anxious and took a bigger bite of the cracker.

"Who is Silas?"

"No one," she muttered.

"Is he your. . . imaginary friend?" Iris pressed.

"No."

She smiled indulgently. "It's fine if—"

"He's not anybody."

"Ok, then," Iris said as if it didn't really matter. "But you don't have to be embarrassed to have an imagin—"

"He's not *imaginary*. He's the boy who lives in the coal room." Mia tossed the cracker onto the floor in her pique. "You can't see *him* either. Not unless you're with me."

Iris forgot to breathe for a moment. She believed in the coal room now, fine. But a boy living down there? That *was* just Mia's imagination. Heck, Mia still believed in the Tooth Fairy. And yet. . . .

"Will you take me to see him?"

"No," Mia said. "I'm mad at him. He was mean to me, and I told him I wasn't going to play with him anymore."

"I just want to see if he's ok. He can't just live down there."

Mia scowled. "He wanted me to bring him upstairs, but I told him I wouldn't. He's really mean."

"If you take me to meet him, I'll tell him to be nicer to you." Mia gave her a narrow look, gauging her sincerity. "Only for a few minutes," said Iris. "So I can see if he's all right. He might. . . need something to eat."

"He doesn't," said Mia, resigned now. "But you can meet him."

Reluctantly she trudged down to the basement, Iris following.

This time the curtain was obvious. Iris almost ran into Mia as she paused and took a deep breath before ducking through.

The room was just as she remembered it, but with one exception.

There was a boy. Just as Mia had said, sitting in the far corner adjacent to the pile of coal. His eyes were sharp and his face suddenly excited by their arrival. It was hard to gauge his age. Iris pegged him at three or four for a moment, then he seemed to age slowly to catch up with Mia.

She goggled.

Silas, for so he must be, was lean and almost translucent pale with dark shadows below his eyes. Dull blonde hair fell past his ears in a limp mop. He wore cut-off jean-shorts and a dirty blue T-shirt, shaded with coal dust.

He stared at Mia with longing, and she slid backward to stand slightly behind Iris.

"I didn't think you were coming back," he said. "Is this your sister?"

"You told him about me?" Iris said, oddly shocked.

"We talked about things," Mia mumbled.

"You shouldn'ta left me for so long," he said. "It's lonely."

"How long have you been down here?" Iris asked.

The boy shrugged. "I'm bad, so I have to stay down here. They don't like me."

"Who doesn't like you?" Iris drew closer and crouched down in front of him. He seemed even smaller when she did so.

"They say I'm bad." He drew a finger through a layer of coal dust on the floor, leaving a line of naked stone behind.

"I don't see how you can be bad. You're just a little boy." But Iris was lying. This boy was bad. Being near him was like watching a friend pour kerosene around an abandoned building.

But he was also fascinating. And what could he do here, alone, in a small, dirty room?

The boy's soft cheeks and sad plump lips didn't quite diminish the cutting and ancient glint in his eyes, but Iris melted all the same when he asked, "Won't you play with me?"

* * * * *

The curtain was not obvious to Iris this time. It was more like one of those strange 3-D images with the swirls and jags of color that revealed itself once you stopped focusing. She walked toward it, finding the curtain with her mind, and letting it brush over her face and shoulder like a mist. She pushed through with cold determination, and found the coal room.

Empty.

Not possible!

"I know you're in here, Silas! Give me my sister!"

Iris flailed, spinning through the room like a dervish, hoping to find him with a blow. She kicked into the corners and pitched clumps of coal against the wall. She might not be able to see him, but surely she could hit him.

Once the initial panic passed, Iris gathered her senses and dropped to the floor. She pulled the largest stone out from the entry of Silas's secret cache, not certain what she was searching for, and found it empty as well.

"I know you're here!"

She beat the stone against the wall in frustration, and a chunk of the mortar cracked and fell to the ground. Scarcely believing what she had seen, Iris, hit the wall again. Stones and mortar fell away under the beating—not easily, but away they came. She dug and scraped to pull out the stones. Her nails chipped and broke, but she didn't pause to suck them.

A sleeping part of her brain noticed that the stones were strangely warm.

Iris gave a mighty blow and a large knob of stone wobbled, and broke away. She heaved it behind her to reveal a gap on the other side. And through the gap came a blast of hot air. It buffeted her face, and the stench curled up into her nostrils. It reminded her of rotten eggs, and she gagged before catching her breath.

"Mia!" The wall came apart easily now, and she clawed at the broken bits, tossing them aside as they came away in her hands. It was the matter of a couple minutes before she had a hole large enough to squeeze through.

She paused, panting. Iris knew no one else could help her. She was the only family member who even had a chance of following Mia now, and still she knew her opportunity may have already passed.

Iris shouldered her way through the gap into the dark, faintly glowing passageway beyond.

"Mia!?" Iris's voice rolled down the rocky corridor and echoed in a space far beyond the coal room.

* * * * *

"What do you want to play, Silas?" Iris asked, settling herself on the floor.

The boy ignored her. "I want you to play too." Silas said, casting a doleful look at Mia who stood watching with her arms crossed.

165

"Why don't you and I play for now. Mia will warm up in a few minutes, ok?"

The boy's lower lip protruded, but he gave a nod of acceptance.

"Can you do tic-tac-toe?" Iris suggested.

Silas shot her a look, took a piece of coal and drew a board on the stony floor. He slashed an X through the center square.

He placed the coal on the floor between them, and Iris put an O in the corner.

"Tie," Silas said after a couple turns. "If both people play right, it's always a tie. I always play right."

"Yeah. Sorry, it was a boring idea. Are you hungry?"

"No."

"How long have you been down here?"

Silas shrugged.

Iris sighed inwardly. The boy probably couldn't be bad in the coal room, but he could be boring.

"Can we play with the top?" Mia suggested, tentatively.

Silas's blue eyes lit at the suggestion. "Sure." He sprung to his feet and collected the string and top from his little store and sat again.

As he wound the string, Iris could see that the top was quite short, probably from being so well used. The peg was worn to a nub on the bottom.

"You go first," he said, and this surprised both Mia and Iris.

Mia gave it a pull, but had the wrong angle and the top bounced on the floor, gave a feeble spin and died.

"I'll show you," Silas said. Under his practiced hand, the top zipped around the room wildly, and Mia grinned. Iris wanted to try it, but she let Silas catch it, rewind it, and carefully put it in Mia's hand. Her pull was good this time, she fixed on it as it twirled past her knees and wobbled on an uneven stone, but Silas had his eyes on something else. When Mia leaned forward to grab the pitching top, Silas pounced, plucking a few stray hairs from Mia's temple.

Iris heard the snatch.

Her sister gave a squawk of pain and scrambled back, and Iris slapped reflexively at Silas's hand.

"You don't pull hair!" she barked at him. There was a smack as their bodies met and both cried out in surprise. Iris jerked her hand away with a yelp and examined her fingertips. It was as if she'd touched a hot burner; white patches rose across the pads of her fingers. *They're gonna blister*, she thought with disbelief. Silas glowered at her, with the back of his hand to his mouth. She wondered if he had been burned as well.

"I just wanted to touch," he said, in a muffled voice.

"No, you pulled it," snapped Mia, already on her feet. "Why did you do that?"

"Whoever put you down here, had the right idea about you," said Iris. "And Mia did too."

Mia snorted. "Told you so."

Iris glared at Silas who looked sulkily at the motionless top. "You could at least say sorry."

"Sorry," he said. But he wasn't really.

"Come on," said Iris. "Let's go." But Mia was a step ahead of her already.

* * * * *

The afternoon Mia disappeared, she and Iris had fought. They had been bickering for most of the day in fact, picking at each other over nothing. Neither had gone into the basement for nearly two months, but Silas was not forgotten. Sometimes the girls talked about him, convincing each other, by turns, that it was better to avoid the coal room. But the matter had just become another point of contention between them. And today, as the storm clouds roiled and churned overhead, there was electricity in the air.

It all came down to a game of *Uno.*

"Draw Four! Blue. Uno." Iris said, snapping the card on the table.

Mia's mouth popped open. "You're a cheater. I don't want to do anything with you anyway."

"You can't just quit because you're losing! You came begging me to play."

"Cause I *wanted* to play—until you cheated!" Mia dropped her fistful of cards and they went sliding. "But I'm not playing with you anymore."

"Terrific! Then we'll both be happy," snapped Iris.

"I'm going downstairs to play with Silas, then," she said with a flounce. "'Cause he doesn't like you either."

That almost stung.

"Fine," Iris said with a scoff. "You might want to put your hair back in a ponytail first."

* * * * *

Carefully, Iris stood upright, and she squinted in the faint red glow that lit the cavern around her. It was a claustrophobic passage only twice as wide as Iris herself, and she tried not to breathe too deeply.

"Mia?" Iris's throat clenched tight. "Mi—"

Iris forced her legs to carry down the path as the fear began clawing at her. The ground was uneven beneath her feet, but she pressed further in. Above her, far beyond the glow, the rocky walls extended an unknowable distance.

Keep going. Keep walking. It grew warmer. Iris sweated. She hated the heat. In the summer, she was always snapping and angry, but now she let the heat-anger feed her wavering courage.

The ground began sloping away gently. Iris felt the muscles in her legs compensate and she had to lean back slightly to stay upright. Down, further down the path she went.

There was sound now. Voices muttered in the distance. She could make nothing of them—those layers of voice hissing and sliding over one another like worms in a bucket. Once she thought she heard laughter behind her, but when she spun, heart racing, there was nothing there but the long, red passage behind her.

"Mia! I'm coming!" Her voice echoed, drowning out the sound beyond her.

She walked faster, jogging now, arms pumping, lungs aching. The walls began peeling away until she could not have touched both sides with her arms outstretched.

Finally, the corridor made a sharp turn and narrowed again. Iris turned sideways and edged her way along, fearing that the walls would collapse too far inward for her to get through. But as it became nearly impassible, she found herself in an open area perhaps twice the size of the coal room above.

And there, sitting beneath a shelf of jutting rock, sat Mia, who looked up at her with dull eyes.

Iris panted, hands on her knees. It was like breathing in acid. Mia raised her head mechanically.

"It's you," she said, her voice toneless. "I'm playing with Silas, and we don't want you here."

Iris started. She hadn't even noticed him at first—Silas who stood across the room, motionless, with eyes as dead as a gargoyle.

"Mia has to stay with me now," he said.

"No, she doesn't. I'm taking her." Iris was across the room in four steps.

"She promised she would stay," said Silas. His voice was deathly calm.

"She was wrong. We're going."

Iris reached down and grabbed her sister's arm, but reeled back with a sharp cry. She gasped and looked down at her burned hand. Mia, too, had started and jerked away, dropping whatever she'd been holding.

They lunged for it at the same time, but Iris was faster.

"Give it back, it's mine!" Mia whined.

It was the coal doll from Silas's cache, but the figure had been transformed from the lump that had once been nothing more than the idea of head, body, legs and arms. Now, it was a work of exquisite detail, and not a thing that could be done by the hands of a child.

And it looked like Mia.

From the stubborn jutting chin, to the high cheek bones, Iris knew the doll the moment she saw it. But what arrested her attention was a knot of curly black hair tied around the doll's neck. Iris fingered it and shivered. *Mia's.*

"That's my doll!" wailed Mia, jumping up and down in fury, but too frightened to touch her sister.

"You can't have that!" Silas screamed.

Iris looked right into his ancient, black eyes.

"Neither can you."

Iris dropped the doll to the floor and stamped hard.

"No!" he screeched.

"Iris!"

The doll crumbled under Iris's foot, and she ground down and dug in, growling with effort.

Silas was the only one screaming now. Mia blinked, halted mid-outrage, and her face twisted into a new expression.

Absolute terror.

"Come on!"

This time, Mia's touch did not burn her, and Iris dragged her sister to the corridor's mouth.

Silas was immobile with rage. "You can't go!" he bellowed after them.

"Scream all you like. You can't touch us. It would burn you up." Iris dragged her sister out of the room. The passage was almost completely dark now, and Iris groped her way forward with her blistered hand.

"I'm *scared*." Mia's voice was choked with tears.

"I know. Just run with me!"

Silas's howls of rage filled the corridor like a flood pressing them forward. Mia tried to run with her free hand over her ears.

The other voices were louder now too, and the stony walls began to shake and buzz. Thread-thin veins of red shone where the cracks appeared, and throbbing heat poured through. Iris was running nearly blind. She pattered one hand along the wall in front of her to find their way. She jammed her fingers again and again and felt the blisters pop.

Soon she could no longer hear Mia crying over the roar of the crumbling walls. Silas's voice rose still louder, and the stones cracked began hailing down upon them. Iris was on the verge of screaming herself.

A slab of mortar fell and struck her temple. She saw stars, felt Mia stumble, but still pressed on.

Just when it felt as if the entire world would collapse upon them, Iris heard a new sound. Not the rumble of rocks, but thunder. The *storm*.

"We're here, honey! We're here." Iris scrambled over a pile of jagged rubble. She dragged herself through the hole in the wall, spun, seized her sister, and pulled her through, as if she were no heavier than her tiny, coal effigy. Behind her, the rocky cavern collapsed.

A blast of hot air followed, with the echo of a scream that had somehow become a laugh.

The girls fell upon each other in exhaustion and fear, as the coal room dissolved around them.

* * * * *

Iris clutched her sister to her and rocked her as she cried.

"It's ok, honey," she murmured, stroking Mia's wet face. "Nothing can get you now. I'm sorry I got mad at you." Iris was shaking and scarcely noticed when Officer Garcia ran over and knelt beside her.

"Where did you find her?"

"She, was. . . stuck." Iris said, swallowing hard.

"Here, let's see you," he said, trying to check Mia over, turning her face in his hands.

Iris wiped her eyes on her shirt, and breathed deeply, trying to clear her nose.

Through her haze of emotion, she noticed it again. The smell of old lightning. The smell of "below," but it was also the smell of something else. Something else leaking from the coal room into the basement.

Iris was on her feet in an instant, dragging Mia up with her. "We have to get out!"

"What?" said Garcia.

"Smell it—that's—"

"Gas leak!" he shouted.

Iris was already spinning away. Mia gave a startled cry as Officer Garcia scooped her up, and they charged up the stairs, Iris taking them two at a time, and Garcia following fast on her heels.

"Got her!" Iris screamed when she reached the landing. "We've found Mia! Run! Get out of the house!" A bang sounded behind her, and she yelped, belatedly realizing it was Officer Garcia slamming the basement door behind them.

She barreled into the living room where her mother spun toward them with desperate eyes.

"Mia!" she screamed, rushing forward to wrest her daughter from the officer's arms.

"No time!" he said to her. "There's a gas leak in the basement!"

"Gas leak?" Her father and Officer Reaves were running down the stairs from the upper floor.

Garcia didn't miss a step but raced toward the front door, looking back to make sure Officer Reaves was herding the rest of the family out from behind.

A blast shook the house, and the porch buckled under Iris's feet as a whoosh of air stripped the breath from her lungs. Officer Reaves gave a shout and stumbled, but Iris and Fritz kept her on her feet.

The rain poured down and the wet grass of the lawn was treacherous under foot, but Iris felt a million miles away. She was only distantly aware of anything beyond the fact that her family was safe and together.

Mia cried in their parents' arms, and Fritz wiped the rain from his face while smoke and debris billowed from their home. Officer Reaves's radio screeched, and two police cars pulled down their tree-lined lane.

Someone put a blanket over her shoulders and said something, but Iris didn't understand the words.

What she heard was one last peal of distant thunder, or maybe it was a dying laugh.

Or it might just have been Iris's imagination.

But soon the fire engines would arrive. And soon the rain would beat the smell of brimstone from the air.

Marvel-less

The day Kenny learned he could fly was the worst day of his life.

It happened during the high school regional football game—the first time the DeForest Cougars had a shot at the state championship in twenty years. There were six seconds remaining, and a touchdown would clench it. The crowd was at full roar, and the ground seemed to tremble with the noise. Kenny was trembling too, and his blood rushed like fire. He was not the largest boy on the team or the fastest. No one was expecting him to carry the ball—and that was why the play was going to work.

Football star. Kenny liked the sound of that quite a bit. He was an average guy of average looks with average smarts. And he knew it. Kenny often thought that, if he had Superhero name, it would probably be "Average Guy." But this play had the potential to make him something special.

"Head in the game," he snapped at himself. "The game is now!"

Kenny shook out his legs as his teammates took up their positions on the two-yard line. Their orange and blue uniforms clashed against the grey and white of the Oregon Falcons on the other side. Kenny lined up in the backfield, to the right of Phelan, their quarterback. Excitement thrummed through him, making him hyper-focused. He was seeing everything, not merely the letterbox view offered him through his helmet. He was almost supernaturally aware of the weakness in the defensive line and how his teammate, Matt, shifted slightly in that direction, preparing to reinforce the block. Every Cougar sensed it. They knew exactly where to put that ball.

Phelan barked the play and received the snap, and Kenny's nervous system lit up. He was in motion before he even made the decision to move.

Years after the game, that was the moment Kenny remembered best—the exact moment the play started, when he heard the first pulse of blood in his head. In fact, it was the last memory he had of the day at all.

The ball came at him in a shuttle pass. Kenny clutched it to his chest and barreled toward the end zone like a rhinoceros. He bellowed through clenched teeth, spinning away from a defender who had slipped past his blocker. Kenny ran at a slant to the line and launched himself over another Falcon, extending the ball with both hands. All that had to happen was for the football to break the plane of the goal. And it did.

The only problem was, Kenny had rocketed himself clean off the ground and was eleven feet in the air when it happened.

Up he went, and forward, carried by his momentum to clear the end zone entirely. As he sailed over the distant fence, the ball fell from his hands, and his arms windmilled in a desperate attempt to control his flight. His crystal-clear vision dissolved to a blur.

The screaming crowd below, already half standing, rose *en masse*, gaping as Kenny blazed an orange and blue trail through the air beyond the visitors stands. Screams turned to cries of horror as he plummeted back toward the earth. Everyone was frozen in shock, except for Kenny who slammed helplessly into the rocky hillside. A trail of dust and debris rose where he tumbled in a whirlwind of limbs for a dozen yards before finally coming to rest.

* * * * *

Kenny rolled his neck and stretched his arms carefully to test them after his uncomfortable sleep. The hospital kept him overnight for observation (unnecessarily, he thought); he felt pretty good, considering.

His mother watched with relief, as well as pride, as the doctor gave him a quick once-over the next morning. She had stayed all night, in spite of Kenny's insistence that he was just fine and that she should go home and get some real rest.

The doctor removed the stethoscope from her ears, and shook her head in amused disbelief as Kenny pulled down his T-shirt. "You sound great," she said. "And your football gear took most of the damage, but even your hands and forearms are still in pretty good shape. And no breaks! That's incredible." Dr. Medlin tapped Kenny's leg with a medical chart. "You've got some Superman in you, I guess."

Kenny's mother blushed and fiddled with her bracelet.

"Don't tell my father that," said Kenny. "My father says Superman's an ass."

The doctor coughed. "I'll have a nurse bring the discharge orders."

Kenny felt bad about mentioning the Superman thing, but he had been thinking all night about his flying failure. He knew his parents already felt the sting of being second-string Superheroes. Sure, they had abilities, but theirs were clearly in a different arena than those of Captain America and Jean Gray and Superman and the like, and the top-rung Supers always let them know it.

All over the world, petty and mid-level villainy was dealt with by local Supers like his family. Only when there was drama or arch-evildoing did the "Über-Supers" deign to make an appearance. And then, they wouldn't even bother to consult with the local crime-fighters at all. They would fly right in and make a nuisance of themselves without so much as checking in with the people who had been monitoring and containing the problem to begin with. More often than not, the Über-Supers wouldn't even accept help from the likes of Kenny's family, who took care to work with finesse and nuance, and tried to minimize the damage wrought by the wild battles and wars waged by Supers who had an image to maintain.

It was the Über-Supers who blasted buildings, ripped up roads, and caused massive destruction in the name of saving the world. Very sexy, of course. But the second string did plenty of good too, just without the devastation.

And yet *who* got all credit? And the comic books? And the movies and the action figures?

Yeah, that's right.

"Why are you scowling?" his mother asked as he bent to tie his shoes. "Are you in pain?"

"No, I'm ok," Kenny said quickly. "No reason."

* * * * *

They were on their way out of the hospital when Kenny's dad suggested a celebratory meal to fête the newest Super.

"I don't really feel like celebrating," Kenny mumbled, blinking in the sunlight. "Not when my teammates can't."

His dad cut him a look, but Kenny brushed it off. Coach Travis and some of his teammates had visited him in the hospital the night before, bearing the bad news. The refs had no idea what to do with the play but eventually ruled it an illegal procedure. "Spontaneous flight on the part of the ball-carrier," they called it.

Final score? Falcons over Cougars, 28 – 23.

"It wasn't your fault," Phelan said. "Any of us could have performed better at any time. It never comes down to a single play." Kenny tried to appreciate the kindly meant platitude, but it grated on him.

Kenny's father, however, felt he should take the statement at face value and had no patience for moping. He clamped a hand to Kenny's shoulder and gave it a firm squeeze.

"Look at the bigger picture, Kenny. You lost a game, but you gained something even greater." Turned out Kenny's shoulder was pretty sore, and he hid his grimace of pain with a nod. "Come on then," his dad said. "Let's go get brunch."

Kenny's dad, Mighty Mouth, was a big fan of brunch, not to mention superpowers. He himself had the strongest head in the world. He could bite through trees, tear cars apart with his teeth, and pound cinderblocks to dust with his forehead. But in his downtime, he preferred quiche.

They pulled into a shabby-looking diner—always the best place to get "real" cooking, according to his father. Kenny's mom requested a table in the corner, a position that typically shielded them from autograph seekers, not that they ever had many to deal with, even when they were in uniform. The waiter didn't even appear to recognize them.

"I just can't believe I have a power," Kenny mused when the waiter had delivered their meals and disappeared again. *I can't believe I suck so bad at it.*

"I knew you'd have one," his mother said. "I'm not surprised at all."

His father looked up from his careful application of powdered sugar onto a cherry blintz. "Your mother's an optimistic woman," he said. "Honestly, I was beginning to wonder." He gave a wink to show he was teasing, but Kenny knew it was only a half-jest.

"Guess you're just a late bloomer," pronounced Ivy as she reached for the maple syrup. Kenny snorted at this. He stole the glass pitcher from under her hand and pretended to pour it over his little sister's head, to her giggling delight. Ivy had found her power this year, too, though she was only seven years old.

"Quit that," chided their mother, as she fought down a smile.

"It's ok," said Kenny. "Maybe she's right. Plus it takes a little time to get used to a power, too. Doesn't it?" He hoped he didn't sound desperate as he eyed his sister who shrugged and blushed. Ivy, a.k.a. Hot-Hands, had accidentally found her power when she was making herself an after-school snack. She popped an entire bag of microwave popcorn and set it on fire before she could even think to drop it. The fake butter made an admirable accelerant, and the result had been a column of flame that scorched the ceiling. The entire kitchen might have gone up in flames if their mother, the Huff, had not been there. She managed to blow out the fire with two enormous blasts of breath.

"It's absolutely true," avowed his mother. "With a little practice, I'm sure you'll be a great flyer."

Kenny was trying to be optimistic, but he had a bad feeling, and his corned beef hash stuck going down. He was torn between excitement at his ability to fly and his dread of ever flying again.

It was mid-morning, and there were only three other patrons in the diner, an elderly couple and a woman who was, perhaps, their daughter. It deserved to be better attended, considering how good the food was.

It was at precisely that moment another pair entered the scene. The man wore a hoody, and the woman had a long, dark coat and a floppy hat that obscured her face.

Her voice was jagged as a rusty razor blade.

"Everyone put your hands up, and there won't be any trouble!" She snapped her arm toward the room, and Kenny's eyes locked on the gun in her hand. She covered the older couple and Kenny's family, swinging the pistol back and forth between them.

The man, too, had a gun, and his was leveled at the hostess. "Open the register and give me everything you got," he barked at the young woman who stared blankly at the barrel of the weapon. "Now!"

The hostess yelped, then hurried to obey.

The female robber wasted no time either. "Toss your bags there on the floor," she said. The elderly woman in the corner looked furious and tossed her bag to the ground with a lemony expression.

Kenny watched as his own mother casually laid her purse on the floor. Kenny's father was following the proceedings with Superhero calm, and Kenny tried to do likewise. "You need to put that weapon down," his father said to the robber as she approached. "If you do, we'll ask the judge to go easy on you."

Across the table, Ivy was pretending to toy anxiously with the pepper shaker. The woman gave her a look but let it go. *Nothing dangerous about pepper,* her expression seemed to say as she picked up the purse. But Kenny saw his mother inhaling slowly, deeply.

"Is that all there is?" the man snarled at the teary-eyed hostess who was now emptying the change out in her apron.

"Folks pay with cards." She sounded apologetic.

The man grabbed the tip jar and was about to drop it into his bag, when Kenny heard the blast of wind from his mother's lungs. On reflex he covered his face and watched the events between his fingers.

A cloud of pepper hit both robbers in the face, the woman first, but the man a scant moment later. It must have hurt—like a sand-blaster to the eyes. The man screamed and flailed with his empty hand. The woman stumbled and threw up her arm to shield herself.

"The money! Bring the money!" she screamed, waving her gun, whose purpose she'd clearly forgotten, as she ran toward the door.

But it was too late. Kenny and his father were already on their feet and after them in a bound. It was a sure thing. . . . Just like last night's touchdown play.

In an unimaginable fluke, Mighty Mouth tripped on a ripple in the rug and went sprawling with a curse. As for Kenny, he was lunging for the woman when he felt the floor pull away. He sliced through the air, ricocheted off the cashier's stand and shot across the room like a shiny BB. Someone was screaming. He skidded through a pile of dirty plates that hadn't yet been collected from an abandoned table and bounced off the far wall before, finally, he collided with the male robber who was still stumbling toward the door. Air exploded from the man's lungs as Kenny plowed into his belly, and they both hit the floor with a crash. Kenny went numb on impact.

He couldn't move at all. The only sensation in his body was the sluggish pulse of blood through his veins. Behind him, the robber gave a faint groan.

His family was all on their feet now, and through the front window, Kenny saw the female robber frozen in mid-stride. A warm breeze came in from the open door and Kenny rolled his eyes, the only part of his body that obeyed him, and stared up at the new arrivals.

One was a black man, a shade lighter than his father, with a smirk on his face and an enormous diamond in one ear. The other was a chubby white guy with shaggy, thinning hair and a face flecked with acne. They surveyed the room with amusement.

"Well, I guess we got here right on time, Slo-Mo," the white guy said to his partner. Kenny tried to speak but couldn't form the words.

"Don't try to talk, boy. You been slo-ified. It'll take you a second to come around. Best just lie still for a moment 'til it passes." The man patted Kenny on the shoulder and rose to make his way toward his family. "Sorry we didn't arrive sooner. Didn't get word about your son until this morning," he explained.

Kenny's father looked hypnotized as he extended his hand to this newly arrived Super.

"Slo-Mo," he said in a raspy voice. "It's been forever, man! Where are you livin' now?"

"It's been a long time, Mighty Mouth. It sure has." Slo-Mo pumped his father's arm, and no one noticed that he failed to answer his old friend's question. "So, I'm sorry to say this is a work visit. We heard about your boy here," he nodded in Kenny's direction, as he was gradually uprighting himself. "There are others like him, you know. Folks with great powers, but they sometimes need special training to control them. The faster your son can learn to control his flight, the better it'll be for him. But he'll need intensive, focused training."

Kenny's body was still tingling faintly, but not painfully, as he walked over to join the conversation. The robber must have been differently slo-ified since he was moving no more quickly than the hour hand on an analog clock.

"Can you train me?" Kenny asked. "Train me to fly?"

Slo-Mo gave him a winning smile. "Sure we can. Flight is a tricky power, and learning the technique in slow motion is better." Kenny's brain was churning sluggishly, but this seemed to make sense. "This here is the Comet," Slo-Mo said, belatedly introducing his partner. "He's got lots of experience with this type of situation."

Comet? Kenny fought to keep the surprise off his face. Really, *Comet*? The guy looked like the front part of a comet, at least. Round and blazing pale. And he seemed to blink too often, but it was hard to imagine the rest of him going very fast.

"We ought to leave right now if this is something you want," Comet said, looking around. The two criminals were still slo-ified to utter incapacitation, but the people at the other table were snapping shots on their phones and making calls. "If you've had two events in the last 24 hours, you need some immediate intervention. It's only been two, right? You aren't hiding any?"

"No! Just two," Kenny replied quickly.

"So, do you want to come?" asked Slo-Mo. "You don't even need to pack. We have everything you need. We can leave right now—er, with your permission, of course, Mighty Mouth."

Kenny felt a surge of excitement not at all tempered by the look his parents gave one another or Ivy's expression as she leaned against their mother, eyes glittering with jealousy.

"Can I go, Dad?"

His father looked a little stunned at the speed with which everything was happening.

"This—this is what you want." It was a statement, but in his father's voice, it sounded like a question.

"More than anything," Kenny said.

His parents gave one another a long look before his mother turned, decision made.

"You take care of our son," she said to Slo-Mo before seizing Kenny in a rib-cracking embrace, which he returned without an ounce of embarrassment.

"We will. You can count on us, ma'am," he said. It was kind of a funny thing to say, Kenny thought, but he could tell his mother liked it.

"It won't take long, will it?' Ivy sniffed, pretending she wasn't about to cry.

"Hard to say." Slo-Mo crouched to look her in the eyes, a Superhero move if ever there was one. "But we'll do everything we can as fast as we can. We won't keep your brother long."

"I'm proud of you, Kenny." His father hugged him quickly and pounded him on the back a couple times for good measure. "We can take care of everything here," he said to the other men, giving a wave of his hand to indicate everything from the slo-ified, would-be robbers, to the stunned employees and clientele, and even the upset diner itself.

"I know you can," said Slo-Mo.

Looking back later, Kenny thought there might have been a shade of derision in his voice.

* * * * *

The next several days made Coach Travis's "man-up" football practices feel like preschool. Kenny wondered if he had made a mistake accepting their offer of training as he staggered into the shade of a leafy tree where Slo-Mo and Comet waited for him.

Everything ached, not just from repeated impacts with the ground and trees, but from Slo-Mo's slo-ification which was beginning to feel like torture. Comet was endlessly patient, though, alternating between exhorting and cajoling, inspiring and menacing, as Kenny went spazing helplessly through the air again and again. Kenny wondered if that was, in fact, Comet's superpower, as he showed no other particular ability. He would have made a helluva football coach, Kenny thought. Unfortunately neither Comet's encouragement nor his commands did anything to improve Kenny's flying.

"I can't do it," he said and collapsed onto a fallen log in the secluded practice field. "I can't. You can't let anyone know. I'll never be able to do it!"

Kenny clutched his head with both hands, on the verge of breaking down. How would he go back to his parents? How would he be able to hide his half-assed "ability" if he took off uncontrollably at some random moment?

"There is one last thing that might work," Comet said thumping a fist on his knee.

"What's that?" Kenny looked up and rubbed a wrist across his leaky eyes.

"This." Comet opened his hand to reveal a tiny, gold smear that Kenny had to blink twice to see clearly. "It's just a prototype, but I'm certain it will work."

"Wh-what is it?" It looked like something his father would have in his collection of antique Superhero memorabilia—but mini-modern. The gold smear now looked like some sort of thin, gold computer chip about the size of his pinkie nail with two long, hair-like wires sticking out from its flat side.

"It's a neurostimulator. I made it," Comet said brusquely, as if warding off an objection, or an exclamation of surprise. "I'm a genius inventor—that's a superpower. Like Iron Man and the Bat Man. What are they but rich guys with fancy inventions?" It sounded to Kenny like he'd been preparing those words for a long time, and Kenny had no intention of gainsaying him.

"Yeah, totally," he agreed fervently. "What does it do?"

Comet gave him a quick grin then. "I can just slip this into the back of your neck, near the brainstem. It will stimulate the synapses in your nervous system that are in communication with your posterior parietal cortex. This will help you make sense of your somatosensory and proprioreceptive. . . " Kenny lost focus here, but came back just in time to hear Comet finish with ". . . help you understand your position in space. I think that's what you're lacking. Figure that out, and you're a flyer."

A prototype? Something new, right? *Brainstem*? A dozen questions might occur to a right-thinking person at this point in the conversation, including: *is it safe*? And *will it hurt*? But Kenny was exhausted, helpless, and desperate.

"When can we put it in?" he asked.

"Right now, if you want."

Kenny let himself react before common sense could trip him up. "Do it. If you think it will help me fly, just do it. Now." He slumped over his knees, revealing his vulnerable neck to Comet and the golden chip.

"Keep still, then." Slo-Mo, ever the cool and dignified presence, stepped forward to settle restraining hands on Kenny's shoulders, and Comet took a centering breath.

The first sensation of the thin wires through his skin was no more uncomfortable than a mosquito bite, but a moment later a storm broke in his head, and he felt his teeth might shatter with the vibrations that roared through his body. Kenny panted as his thoughts blurred, and he stomped his feet in anguish. He would have screamed, but he dreaded the buzz of his own voice in his head. The only thing more frightening than the sudden onslaught of sensation was its dramatic and utter stop. Kenny thought he had gone deaf and blind, and it took him a moment to realize he was actually seeing, and even looking at Slo-Mo's extended hand. He took it, and Slo-Mo pulled him to his feet.

"Try now," Slo-Mo said. "Fly."

Kenny looked to Comet, who gave him a careful nod as he rose to his feet. He felt dreamy, like his body was not his own, and his head was cloudy, but he tried anyway. He started at a slow jog then punched off the ground as if he was doing the long jump, and he was in the air again. But this time, instead of sailing into the atmosphere or smashing into a tree, saved only by Slo-Mo's power, Kenny drifted.

He bobbed and listed from side to side. Then he began paddling, trying to get his balance against the thin air.

"Go, go!" shouted Comet.

"I got this! I got this!" Kenny yelled. He began an awkward crawl stroke, swimming through the stillness eight feet above the ground. It took ferocious effort, and his heart felt like it would explode, but he was definitely flying. He climbed higher, paddling and kicking to increase his speed as he began an unsteady right-hand turn.

Below, Slo-Mo chuckled and clapped his heavy hands with admiration. "That's it! That's it, Kenny!"

Kenny blinked down and was surprised to see his friends far below, high fiving one another. He found his position and turned a flip in the air, bellowing with triumph. "You did it, Comet!"

"*You* did it, Kenny!" Comet gave a laughter-punctuated whoop and punched the air like a wild man. Kenny flew until he was so spent he fell out of the sky, saved only by Slo-Mo's quick reaction.

* * * * *

Over the next few days, Kenny couldn't be in the air enough. He made a few bobbles here and there, but nothing had ever felt better—or taxed him more. It wasn't at all like he imagined it. Flying, in his dreams, had been as effortless as breathing, but the reality was more like swimming through Play-Doh. Hovering was easy enough, but maneuvering was agony; however, once he built up some speed, he was a shark in the air.

I'm a flier. I'm a flier! Kenny repeated this mantra in his mind, savoring it over long minutes; he couldn't wait for others to know it, too.

"When can I show my parents?" he asked his trainer-friends. Kenny imagined his mother's delight and Ivy's shrieks as he carried her into the air, not too high or too fast, though. He didn't have the strength for that yet.

"Soon," Comet promised. "Just a few more days. You don't want to leave us so soon, do you?"

"Not really," he admitted. Kenny enjoyed the insouciant bachelor life, two states distant from his responsibilities. He didn't mind putting off school for another week, flying all afternoon, and gaming until he fell asleep every night. Beyond that, there was only one thing Kenny wanted to do, and that was put his superpower to work.

Slo-Mo shook his head, and Comet set his jaw at this. "We promised to keep you safe," they reminded him. "We can't ensure that if you're with us when we're working." And so, night after night, Kenny was left to simmer in the hot tub and rub his muscles with Tiger Balm while Comet and Slo-Mo went to Super it up.

One evening, however, several days after his first flying success, Kenny noticed the back-up police scanner lying forgotten on the kitchen counter.

"Ok, then. Let's hear what's happening," Kenny mused aloud. The answer, as it turned out, was "not much." He let the scanner scratch and announce uninteresting events in the background while he sat down for a *Mass Effect* binge. Just before 11:00 though, as Kenny's eyes were glazing over, he heard the screech of an emergency coming from the handset.

"Possible break-in at FrontierForward Lab. Research Campus East," announced the practiced-sounding dispatcher. This was followed quickly by several responders, and Kenny dropped his controller and turned the scanner up.

"You gonna jump in on this?" Kenny said, to his absent companions. But then he remembered they'd planned on being in the South End that night, and FrontierForward, a high-tech development lab, was on the far northeast edge of the city. Which, come to think of it, was not far at all from the condo in which he was now sitting.

Kenny flew, not literally, to his feet, jumped into a pair of dark jeans, pulled on a gray windbreaker, and was out the door telling himself, "I'll just keep a bird's-eye view on the situation. The eye in the sky." *Right.*

He flew as quickly as he could, keeping to the dark above the glare of the streetlights below. He spied the five-story building now lit by the whirling red and white lights of the emergency vehicles, and took a sweep around it, watching several officers and cars maneuver themselves into position on the ground. Fortunately, not a soul looked up. No one was paying attention to him or the open window on the 4th floor. It would be foolish for him to not go in, really, he decided.

Kenny had some experience with guided landings, Comet and Slo-Mo had improvised obstacles with Hula Hoops and pool noodles for him to fly through and around, but a window was a different matter. He scraped his backside, nearly dragging his pants off his butt against the upper-edge of the window frame, and managed to stop himself against the opposite wall and drop to the floor.

At least I didn't ricochet, he thought, rubbing his back and getting his bearings. He imagined he could hear footsteps, but they disappeared when he peeked out the office door. Faint lights, like the strip on the floor of an airplane glowed from the corners down a long hall. A qualm of fear flipped his stomach, but his Superhero inclination said, *Well, as long as I'm here. . . .*

He crept his way down the hall, hearing the hum of distant equipment and irregular noises he couldn't identify. He tried every glass-paneled door lining the corridor, but found each locked tightly, until he came to the last one. It was already ajar, and it gave so easily under his hand that he actually stumbled. He drew up in a room filled with tidy assembly stations and tables lined with impossible looking components. More monstrosities of metal and wire lined the walls, but in the gray-blue darkness only one thing caught his eye. A red glow on a far table. It was so out of place that Kenny was immediately drawn toward it.

Can't be, he breathed. It was tangle of wires about the size of an old computer hard drive. And on it was a digital display where vicious red numbers were counting down.

21. . . 20. . .

No. No way! Kenny recoiled, then forced himself forward again, his decision made in that split-second. He snatched up the device—it was heavier than he thought—and spun to see a security guard standing in the doorway.

"Put that down and step away from it!" The woman barked at him.

"B-but it's a bomb!" he began.

Her eyes popped wide and she went for her gun, apparently thinking the bomb had been his big idea. "Put it down!" she demanded.

"I can't! Look," he choked out, clutching certain death against his chest. "See? It's counting down." He scuttled toward her, tipping the device so that the red glow of *15* then *14* shone on the woman's horrified face.

"Stop. Stop *there!*" But Kenny could see her confidence waver behind the pistol.

That was all the give he needed.

"Out of the way!" He shot her a stiff arm to the collarbone, and she fell backward as he blasted past. "Sorry!"

"Get back here!" she yelled, scrambling to her feet. "Hey, *Stop!*"

Kenny raced down the hall and leaped through the open window as the woman behind him screamed in horror. The last thing Kenny heard as he lumbered into the sky was her terrified "Nooo!" and then the gurgle as it caught in her throat. He climbed laboriously upward and tossed a look over his shoulder to see her pale face peering out the window at him. Beyond, on the ground below, he caught sight of two dark forms, like shadows, running for the wooded area on the side of the building, untouched by the lights in vast parking area. But he couldn't do anything about that now.

The device thrummed against Kenny's chest, and he peeked down at the glowing numbers as they counted down. "Go, *go!*" He pushed himself harder as the air roared past his ears and the buildings grew smaller below. He was almost dizzy with the speed, and the muscles in his lower back threatened to cramp.

Surely he was high enough now.

4. . . 3. . .

Kenny bellowed as he heaved the bomb as far as he could. Two scant seconds later, the air ripped past him with the force of the blast. His head snapped back, and he tumbled head-over-heels through the air as pinpricks of light danced before his eyes.

He had done it, saved the building. Saved lives maybe. But he felt empty, and he let himself drift until his legs and back begin to tremble. He pieced his thoughts together as spotlights scanned the sky for him, illuminating pieces of the bomb drifting like ash and confetti.

How stupid am I?

Eventually, he dragged himself back to the condo, bracing himself for the confrontation to come.

* * * * *

They were waiting for him in the living room. Slo-Mo was leaned back in the recliner, eyes-closed, and Comet was fiddling with something on the tablet in his lap, but Kenny could tell they had been waiting for him.

Despite the cold night air, Kenny was sweating with anger.

"I trusted you!" he spat.

"And your trust was well placed. Don't you think?" Comet said, setting aside his tablet. "We said we'd help you fly."

"What the *hell* were you doing tonight? I saw you slinking out of the lab!" The bland expressions on his friends' faces only fueled his fury. "So, what. You're cowards. . . You're thieves?" He scraped a brutal hand through his black braids. "A bomb?! *Comet?* You could have killed somebody!" He was shaking with the strength of his disgust. "You could have brought down the building!"

Comet snorted. "Not a chance. So, it made some noise. Threw off some light. All sound and fury, signifying nothing. I wasn't going to make something that would hurt you." Comet played it cool, but was clearly proud of himself. "I had to convince Slo-Mo that twenty-one seconds would be plenty of time. I programmed the counter to start as soon you opened the door." He looked to Slo-Mo who tipped his head in respectful acknowledgement.

"Why and *what* were you steal—Wait, hurt *me?* How did you. . .?"

Comet and Slo-Mo waited for things to really sink in, and Kenny went dead cold.

"I was your dupe? You *used* me?" It all made sense then. The forgotten scanner. The open window. The direct line to the bomb.

"Just tonight. We used you for your own good," Slo-Mo was as calm and velvet-voiced as ever. "And we have a good explanation."

Kenny dropped onto an ancient recliner, anger quenched as if he'd been blasted with a fire hose. "You're—you're not Supers."

Slo-Mo gave him a small grimace. "Never said we were Supers, Kenny. You came to that conclusion all by yourself."

"Sure, because my Dad *knew* you. And plus. . . you-you've been my *friends*!" It was unbelievable. They had tried so hard to help him. They had encouraged him. He thought that meant something. Didn't that make them the good guys?

"Supers aren't the only ones to have friends," said Comet.

Kenny rubbed his face.

"Do you know what we've been doing tonight?" said Slo-Mo gently.

"Of course I don't. Other than lying to me!"

Comet rolled his eyes. "So dramatic," he said. "Tonight we got the materials I need to make your permanent chip."

Kenny was blank.

Comet scratched at his prematurely receding hairline. "Look, the chip you have now is already deteriorating; it was just a first model. You'll need something permanent, and I got the materials I needed tonight. Thanks to you for your own part in that, of course." He gave Kenny a short salute. "I'll finish up with the implantable chip, and then we'll to go Gimmick's lab to implant it. It's going to be a more invasive procedure than with the temporary chip, so we need a safer place to perform it," he rubbed his hands together greedily. "And Gimmick gave us an open invitation when we sent him your before-and-after videos."

"We make a good team," said Slo-Mo.

"Gimmick?" Kenny croaked, hearing the name of one of the greatest mid-level inventor Villains he knew. "Team? Sending videos of me without my permission? I don't even know if I want something in my brain!"

"You want to fly, right? You'll be *fine*. You trust me, don't you?" Kenny glared at him. "Uh, don't answer that right now. Give it some thought first."

"But not too much thought," said Slo-Mo, "It's an easy decision."

"For you."

"For *anyone*," Comet argued. "You get to *fly*. Plus, you can keep the Super-reputation if that's what you really want. You'll have some press tomorrow, I imagine. We can keep going just like tonight. Slo-Mo and I will do what we need to, and you can just run interference. Taking credit however you want."

A sudden, wild hope seized Kenny just then. "What's to keep the Supers from making a chip for me?" he demanded. "If I tell them there's a technology that can give me control of my power, they can develop one too!"

It seemed like the obvious thing, but his companions didn't even twitch.

"Go ask them, then," Slo-Mo said. "Ask the Supers for a brain chip. See what it gets you."

Kenny's stomach curdled. He could easily imagine the humiliation of crawling to the Über-Supers, begging them to create an implantable prorpio-brain-thingy for him. They had no time to spare for a guy like him—a failure even among the second-string Supers. Only the second-string Bad Guys had seen something in him.

"Come on, man. This is a no-brainer. You'll have everything you want, right? You'll fly. You'll have the recognition. You'll be the maverick Super!"

"And *you'll* have it too. A reputation, I mean," countered Kenny. "Among the V-Vi. . . ." He couldn't bring himself to say the word.

"The Villains? The Bad Guys?" Comet offered. "It's okay to say it, Kenny. We're proud of it! And now, we'll get the attention we deserve."

"Villains," Kenny said with a groan. "That's why you helped me? So you could rise in the ranks?"

"'Course we benefit. Tit-for-tat, man! You get what you want, we get what we want," countered Slo-Mo. It was the first time Kenny had ever heard him on the edge of anger. "Everyone benefits."

"*I'm* going to have access to some of the most exquisite equipment on the planet," Comet was practically buzzing with excitement.

No such thing as altruism, Kenny thought morosely.

"Come *on*! What more can you want?" pressed Comet.

Kenny rubbed his face hard. That was a good question.

* * * * *

Kenny swooped as swiftly as he dared and slid Ivy carefully to the ground in his parents' back yard.

"Ta-da!" he sang. Ivy danced and pumped her arms as if she had done the flying herself while their parents applauded.

"We knew you could do it," said their mother, tiptoeing to press a kiss to Kenny's cheek and handing him a glass of sweet tea.

It hadn't been easy to convince Slo-Mo and Comet to let him come home for a final visit. Settling into a porch chair, on the back porch, he understood why. It was a modest bungalow filled with his mother's books and houseplants, his father's embarrassing, though mostly functional, collection of old Super memorabilia and obsolete equipment, and his sister's busy energy. This was his place, and this was his family. It would easily break him, if he weren't so determined.

"So, who all have you met? A lot of other Supers stop in there?" his dad asked. He was laboring under Kenny's carefully constructed fiction that he was training at some sort of remedial Super training compound.

Kenny shrugged uncomfortably. "Nah. We're trying to keep everything real close to the vest. They didn't want any distractions or anything."

"Perfectly sensible," his mother said. "You might get the idea to show off or take chances you don't need to take when you're just learning."

This rubbed Kenny the wrong way, but he didn't think he could correct her without showing his hand. He had to play it smart.

"What'cha gonna call yourself?" asked Ivy.

"How about a sort of helicopter name?" suggested his father. "What do you think about Chopper? That's a good one. Better than Whirleybird," he added after sudden inspiration. "Plus, it kinda goes with mine. Super-heroing as a father-son business, hey? Wait, I guess that's Chomper. Nevermind."

Kenny scratched a bug bite on his neck. "Yeah, maybe. I don't know."

"What's wrong?" his mother asked, putting aside her drink. "What aren't you telling us?"

Kenny felt strangely weak. He had wanted to broach this himself. He had prepared the lie well, even choosing his own segue line, but now that was no longer an option.

Kenny sighed. "It's just that. . . I've decided to stay for more training. With Slo-Mo and Comet." He couldn't look at his parents as he lied to them, so he focused on Ivy instead. He watched her face drain, and she looked down at her bare feet and wiggled her toes. Kenny felt like squirming.

"You've made your decision then. Just like that," his father said with a snort. "I notice you didn't exactly ask."

"You need to finish school," said his mother. "We've always told you how important school is!"

"I'll have tutors, there. Just for me," Kenny said.

"So. You think you're going off to play in the big league," said his father. "With the real Supers?"

Kenny felt like he'd been slapped. "No! It's not like that."

"He doesn't mean that, Kenny" his mother said quickly, shooting a look at her husband.

Even this short sniping was too much for Ivy after hearing her brother's bombshell. She began sniffing and sobbing quietly.

"Aw, I'm sorry," Kenny said, reaching toward her. "I'd be going to college next year anyway." His chair nearly fell back when Ivy threw herself at him and squeezed him with all of her strength. Kenny was so caught up that he almost forgot to be afraid of her hands, and he came close to breaking down and confessing everything.

Eventually, after a tense conversation and a few honest tears, Kenny managed to extricate himself from his family for a few private minutes. In his bedroom, he pulled a sheet of a paper from an old spiral notebook, penned a few lines, folded it over and wrote "Mom and Dad" on the outside.

Kenny tapped his note thoughtfully against his mouth before propping it on his dresser and walking out of his home for perhaps the last time.

* * * * *

"I hope you understand," Slo-Mo said, securing the blindfold around Kenny's head. "We need to be certain of your allegiance before you can know where the lab is located."

"Yeah. No problem," he agreed, but he started with a jerk when bag slid over his shoulders. They were taking this very seriously. Kenny swallowed hard, relieved they didn't pat him down, or do something even more invasive.

After an excruciating car ride, Kenny was maneuvered into a helicopter. Not being able to see made the flight a punishment. It didn't feel nearly as good as being in the air on his own, and he was sweating with the effort it took him to not throw up.

Finally, the helicopter settled and the blade noise let up; he heard Comet yell, "Here we are!"

Kenny's head ached in the sudden sunlight as the bag and blindfold were removed. He squinted around him, amazed at the modern lab made of enormous planes of dark glass. Maybe they were only mid-level Villains, but their lab looked pretty darn good, anyway. The building was a bizarre intrusion in an isolated valley. The environment was semi-arid with dust-colored bushes and rocky hillsides on all sides. Where *was* he?

He was walking on trembling legs as they approached the building. Comet chuckled and patted him on the back as a rat-faced little man emerged from the building and marched toward them.

"Slo-Mo. Comet," Gimmick said, not even glancing in their direction. His eyes were fixed on Kenny, and Kenny's on him.

He was small and wiry, with a jutting head, and he made sharp, little actions, like an over-caffeinated ferret. "You're an excellent flier," he said abruptly. "Good speed, plus you can turn on a dime. Superman's turnaround time is crap."

Kenny forced a smile. "Yeah, thanks."

"Let's not waste any time here either. I'm already prepared for you," he said, seizing Kenny by the arm and maneuvering him toward the building. Gimmick wasn't going to give him a chance to back out; that much was certain.

The lab was amazing. Modern in every way, glass and machinery and inscrutable devices, right out in the open, not locked away like in FrontierForward. Unfortunately, it looked almost abandoned today. Perhaps most of the other Villains were out on some crime spree. That was bad luck.

There must have been millions of dollars worth of equipment here. Looking at it as he passed quickly by, Kenny felt he had made the right decision. He really wanted a chance to explore, but the little man tugged him along with fingers like claws. It was amazing how fast he could walk. Gimmick led them into an area somewhat partitioned off from the main room by sophisticated hospital equipment: a glowing sterilizer, confusing-looking monitors, and gadgetry that looked more like gaming consoles than anything with a medical use.

"Have a seat and settle in," Gimmick said, and Kenny climbed into an adjustable chair that might have been more suitable for a space ship. "This will take a while, so I need to put you to sleep."

Kenny hadn't expected this—though he should have—and he jerked involuntarily.

"No! No way!"

Gimmick ignored him and admired Comet's implantable chip under some sort of precision light. "It will not take long to remove the temporary one, and I will slip this beauty right in. It's a nice piece," he said in an aside to Comet. "But you must definitely be out. It's an invasive process. In your *brain*." He banged a finger on Kenny's temple.

"I don't want to be put to sleep!" Not *that*. That would ruin everything! Kenny was halfway out of the chair, but Slo-Mo already had restraining hands on him.

"Easy now. There's nothing to worry about. Gimmick's never killed anyone—at least not anyone on the table," he said with a wink.

Kenny breathed heavily through his nostrils, collecting his courage and wondering if he had made a mistake. "H-how long is it supposed to take, to remove the old one?" he asked, thought whirling.

"The entire process will take no longer than a couple of hours," Gimmick said brusquely, arranging some unpleasant looking tools on a shiny metal tray.

"I don't want to be out that long! How long does the *removal* take?" The clock on the wall read 2:30. How long? *How long?* Kenny asked himself. "If it's such a short time, then it doesn't matter!" He was practically panting with fear. "Comet put it in without any problem. I didn't have to be asleep for that. You keep me awake for that part, then put me to sleep after."

Gimmick ground his teeth and looked at him darkly over a tiny, glinting pick hook.

"Give him a break," Comet said to Gimmick. "Just do this one thing. Let's not humiliate him."

"Fine," Gimmick spat. "I'll remove the temporary, using just a local. Then, *out you go!* Even if you fight me on it, I'll win. I have my ways."

"Sounds fine." Kenny managed a faint smile, but it was short-lived. Even with the local anesthetic the extraction hurt far more than the insertion did. He didn't think Gimmick was trying to be gentle.

"And there is it," Gimmick said, when the first procedure was finished. Lightning raced down Kenny's spine as he turned to see, and he felt a stream of blood trickle down his neck. Between the teeth of the medical tweezers, the temporary chip glinted in the light; its thread-like pathways shone silver and gold, smeared with the deep red of his blood.

Gimmick dropped the chip onto a tray with a click. "Out you go, then. Restrain him for me, you two," Gimmick said, and Slo-Mo and Comet started toward him.

Nope. Kenny thought, fighting off the pain. *Let's do this.*

Summoning every ounce of his strength, Kenny threw himself off the chair and rebounded from the floor, angling his launch past his friends and toward the bewildering machinery. The air whistled past as he took flight, and his foot caught the edge of one of the medical machines, topping it over. Kenny left it, and his own stomach, behind as he tore through the air.

It was simultaneously terrifying and a relief. Kenny had feared he wouldn't ricochet as before, but he was his pre-chip self again, helpless and nearly inured to pain as he crashed off surfaces and careened into bewildering machinery. Weapons and other more incomprehensible devices toppled on impact, spraying parts all over the dark, slate floor.

"Kenny!" Comet bellowed.

"Stop!" Gimmick shrieked.

But Kenny couldn't stop. He had never gone so fast. His mind blurred. He heard the shouts of the men below him and felt the near-blast of Slo-Mo's slo-ifying ray as it missed him again and again.

Kenny's last thought was how glad he was to have left the letter for his parents. He hadn't wanted it to come to this, but he knew it might.

He had no idea how long he'd been banging around when he saw himself sailing toward the enormous glass partition that protected a two-story machine that looked like either a laser or a telescope, perhaps both. He squeezed his eyes shut and covered his face with his arms as he sailed into it. The glass exploded on impact, and Kenny thought he, too, was coming apart.

He hit the ground, breathless, and glass like diamonds hailed down upon him as Kenny gave in to the darkness dragging him away. He couldn't move. He could see only crackles of light behind his closed eyelids, and hear only a wild screaming in his head that grew louder and louder, but he couldn't bring himself to care about it. At some point, he realized the shrieking wasn't in his head but was the sirens of emergency vehicles arriving on the scene.

Kenny didn't have the energy to open his eyes until he felt a hand on his chest and a face pressed to his neck. When he made the effort, he was both bewildered and overjoyed to see his mother above him.

"You read my letter," he croaked.

"You should have told us! Of all the stupid things!" Her face looked aged in a way he had never seen before.

"I told you how to find me. I took dad's old GPS pill."

"You couldn't know whether that old GPS pill would work or not. You had no way of knowing if we'd get here on time."

"No," he admitted. "But I *did* know you'd never let me do this if I'd asked."

"Of course we wouldn't!" Her voice was cracking now, and Kenny wanted to touch her face, but he didn't have the energy to move his arm. "It was a stupid risk, Kenny. *Stupid.* You could have just told us about Slo-Mo and Comet."

His head was thick. He wasn't sure he'd ever be able to explain it. He'd had to do something, and he didn't want to take out Slo-Mo or Comet. Not if he could take out the lab instead. And if he could put the hurt on more important Villains and take out some new Villain weaponry in the process, maybe it wouldn't come out so badly for his less-nefarious friends.

His father's hand appeared on her shoulder.

"Easy on him, hon," he said.

Kenny watched, distantly, as the EMTs put in an IV line and carefully maneuvered him onto a gurney. In the background, PuttyWoman, a family friend, hauled Slo-Mo ineluctably away as he bucked and struggled against her tacky, doughy arms. He heard Gimmick snarling and swearing, but never caught sight of him again.

Kenny wondered where Comet was, but he didn't want to ask. Maybe he'd gotten away. His heart lifted at that, but then he felt bad about it. Comet was a Villain. He deserved to be caught. Didn't he?

Kenny felt very tired. The passing of the adrenaline rush had left him weak and cold, and his muscles were beginning to protest their recent abuse. He thought he had probably broken some bones this time.

The gurney jerked as the EMTs hauled it into position, and Kenny felt himself drifting further away, but there was something he needed to say before succumbing to unconsciousness.

"I know what I want," he said, squeezing his mother's hand.

"What, honey? Anything."

"I want to do the right thing." Kenny said. He could see the confusion in her eyes, but she was quick to agree.

"I'm so proud of you," she said. "You *did* do the right thing."

"And . . . something else."

"What's that?" His father leaned in close to hear him.

"I know what I want my name to be." Kenny was fading hard now, and was only faintly aware of the amusement now lighting his father's face.

"What is it, then?"

"Pinball," he rasped. "I want to be called Pinball."

His mother gave a choked chuckle, and his father gently patted his chest.

"Pinball." He snorted. "That's a good one, son. That's a real good one."

An EMT's face hove back into view then.

"Let's get you fixed up, Superhero," she said, as the gurney began rumbling toward the door. "By the looks of this place, I suppose we should be glad you're one of the good guys, huh?" The ceiling and what remained of the walls passed blearily through Kenny's vision until he could no longer keep his eyes open.

One of the good guys, Kenny thought.

Yeah, he liked the sound of that.

Polly Plays Possum

The following story is a bit of a departure from the others, and I decided to add it to this collection at the last minute. This is the text from a picture book that I really hoped would come about. Being that I read my own children such disturbing fairy tales as "Molly Whoopie" and "The Hobyahs" when they were little, I didn't really think "Polly" was pushing any boundaries. My agent, however, was concerned about "grownup reactions" and whether the subject matter was appropriate for young children, so it's been moldering on my hard drive for years. I love "Polly", and I hope you'll forgive my self-indulgence for including her here.

Mother Possum had raised twenty-seven children, so she knew just when to have "the talk" with her daughter Polly.

"It's a dangerous world for possums, Polly. What with cars and trucks, and bobcats and owls," said Mother Possum.

Polly nodded solemnly. She knew all about the rumbling cars that could mash little possums flat, and the lurking bobcats who just loved possum soup for dinner.

"Whenever you're really in trouble and you don't know what to do, you just play dead," Mother told her. "Flop right over, Polly, and close your eyes, and everyone will leave you alone. It's your special trick. The special trick of our whole family."

"Oh, really Mama?" Polly's tiny pink ears tingled with excitement at knowing the special trick of possums.

"Yes," Mother Possum said with a smile. "Nothing to put off your enemies like being dead."

"Woo-Hoo!" Polly shouted. She couldn't wait to try it and, luckily, she had her chance the very next day.

The school bus bounced along the road and inside, Polly and her friends, Lisa Rabbit, Marcus Robin, and Ralphie Turtle were playing catch with an acorn.

Mr. Coyote, the driver, was grumpy.

"Be quiet back there!" he growled, but no one listened. Everyone laughed and hollered as the acorn flew between the seats. Polly snatched it from the air with her clever paw and tossed it to Marcus Robin, but she accidentally tossed it too high. The fat nut sailed right past Marcus's outstretched wing feathers and smacked Mr. Coyote on the back of the head.

The bus stopped with a screech and Mr. Coyote leaped from his seat. "Who hit me with that acorn?" he snarled. Mr. Coyote's ear flicked back, and his eyes landed right on Polly with a deadly glare. Without even thinking, Polly flopped down on the bus floor with her eyes closed and tried not to breathe.

No one moved for a full minute.

"Oh, no! Polly!" screamed Lisa.

"You killed her, Mr. Coyote! You scared her to death! It's your fault!" Ralphie cried.

Mr. Coyote hopped from foot to foot, one paw in his mouth, looking very scared.

"I didn't mean to do it! Please don't tell anyone. I'll lose my job!"

Mr. Coyote drove very fast up to the school. He carried Polly out of the bus and laid her on a bench by the front door. Then Mr. Coyote jumped back into the bus and sped away as Polly's friends cried.

Polly lay quietly for a few moments, enjoying the attention, before she finally opened an eye.

"Is he gone?"

"Ach!" chirped Marcus.

"You're all right!" cried Lisa, bouncing for joy.

"It's my special trick!" Polly explained. "I get to use it whenever I'm really in trouble and don't know what to do. Mama said so!"

"Ohh!" cooed all her friends.

"I have a special trick too," said Chet Skunk. "Wanna see?"

No one did.

School was great! Mama had packed a delicious, stinky fish in Polly's lunch box; there was a fire drill right in the middle of naptime, so no one had to rest; and when Mrs. Squirrel announced a pop quiz in math class, Polly knew just what to do.

Thud.

She landed on the floor beside her desk and lay perfectly still. This time, Polly let her tongue dangle out of her mouth, too, just for dramatic effect.

Lisa Rabbit snickered.

"Oh no!" wailed Ralphie Turtle. He remembered Polly's trick and was clever enough to see the usefulness in playing it up. "I guess the quiz was too much for her, Mrs. Squirrel." He put his hand to his head and winced. "And I'm not feeling too good myself."

Mrs. Squirrel stared at Polly and wrung her tail between her paws. "I didn't do it on purpose! It was an accident!" Her voice quavered as if she was about to cry. "Whatever will I do?"

Marcus Robin laid a sympathetic wing on his teacher's shoulder. "Don't worry, Mrs. Squirrel. We'll take care of her."

And they did.

Lisa, Ralphie, and Marcus carried Polly away from the school where no one could see her, and she spent the rest of the afternoon making a necklace of red maple leaves.

Polly loved her special trick! She just wished the bus and the classroom had softer floors. Falling down had bruised her a little bit.

* * * * *

After school let out, Polly met her friends in the pasture where they liked to play soccer with a horse chestnut.

"Wow, you sure have a great trick," sighed Marcus.

"Yeah, I do," Polly agreed.

"I don't think we're ever gonna have a test again," said Ralphie. His voice was full of admiration, and Polly blushed.

Suddenly, a large shadow swept over the field. All the animals looked up and froze in fear.

"Hawk!" screamed Lisa. She bounded into a bush in the blink of an eye.

Marcus chirped with terror and flapped into an oak tree.

Ralphie just disappeared into his shell.

And Polly?

Polly played dead.

The black bird dropped and landed heavily next to Polly, and she forced herself to stay still, even though she was very scared and the grass tickled her nose.

If Polly had opened an eye, she would have seen that the bird was not a hawk but a fat, stupid vulture.

The vulture sniffed lazily through his long, sharp beak. He poked at her with a knife-like claw. It hurt, but Polly didn't make a sound. She was playing dead better than she ever had before.

But what Polly didn't know is that vultures only eat dead animals.

"Hmm," mumbled the vulture. "It's a little too fresh, but it'll taste alright, I s'pose."

The vulture splayed his deadly claws and wrapped them slowly around little Polly. They closed tighter and tighter, until Polly found it hard to breathe. He nipped at her neck with his vicious beak.

It was then Polly knew for sure the bird meant to eat her.

Polly opened her eyes and gave a screeching growl as only a possum can, and she snapped at the bird's scaly foot. The vulture started, dropped Polly, and hopped back, confused.

"Huh? Hey, is this some kind of trick, or sumtin?"

"Yes!" shouted Polly. "It's my *newer* trick." Polly bristled so all her hair poked up like hay stubble, and she bared her yellowing teeth and snarled. The vulture flapped his wings as he staggered back. They were so strong it made a wind in Polly's face and buzzed her whiskers.

"No need to be so cranky," groused the bird, "I'm going."

Polly hissed and spat in triumph even as the vulture flew away. Marcus, Lisa, and Ralphie burst out of hiding and cheered.

"Wow! You showed him, Polly," exclaimed Marcus.

"Now that's *really* a trick," said Lisa.

"Yeah. Yeah that *was* pretty good," replied Polly. She meant to sound brave, but her voice was shaking.

When Polly arrived home, Mother and Papa Possum were reading lots of pretty cards with flowers on them. But they didn't seem very happy.

"Look who's alive and well," said Papa.

Mother gave her a narrow look. "Can you tell us why we got these sympathy cards from your teachers today? They seem to think. . . that you were. . ." Even though Mama Possum was angry, she blinked back tears, and Papa gave her a little squeeze.

Polly shrunk into herself. "I showed them my special trick," she said in a whisper.

Papa coughed into a handkerchief, but it sounded like a laugh too.

"Well, you'll have to apologize to everyone tomorrow. And no playing dead to get out of it."

"Oh, rats," Polly grumbled.

It was hard for Polly to face Mr. Coyote and Mrs. Squirrel, but she managed.

"Hrm," Mr. Coyote growled, baring a bright fang in her direction. "Never do it again. And no more throwing acorns on the bus."

And when Polly went to math class, Mrs. Squirrel was so surprised she fell on the floor, and the principal had to administer smelling salts. Mrs. Squirrel went home early that day, and Ms. Mouse came to substitute, and *she* made them write lines and stay in through recess to review their fraction facts.

Mother Possum sat Polly down again that night and explained that she should only use her trick when she was really, *really* in trouble, and that the rest of the time, she should face her problems like a big girl Possum. So, Polly almost never plays dead any more, just when she sees an eagle or a hungry bobcat, or when Mother Possum asks her to wash the dishes.

ACKNOWLEDGMENTS

This book is the result of a decade of short-story writing, and I've racked up so many people who deserve my thanks in this publication that I fear I'll forget some.

I'm thankful first and foremost to my wonderful husband Phil and my four ornery children who share me with the computer.
Thanks to my parents, Barry and Clara, who, when I told them I meant to take up writing, bought me a laptop for Christmas.
A *huge* "thank you" to the many friends who have answered my questions and read, polished, edited, and generally beat these stories into shape with me: Amy Whitlock, Sarah Dodson-Knight, Fatima Shmulsky, Stephanie O'Malley, and Andrea Reichert to name just a few.

To K.C. Dyer, Kathy Chung, Rose Holck, Marsha Skrypuch, and others from the Compuserve forum and the fine "par-*tays*" at the Surrey International Writers Conference

Thank you, Susan D. Cook, for the keen eye, the excellent editing, and the grammar rants.

Thank you, Grace A. Griffin, for every beautiful thing in this book that isn't a word.

And finally, my deep and abiding affection to my friend and mentor, writer Shelagh Lynne Supeene, who has encouraged me from my very first paragraph, lo those many moons ago.

ABOUT THE AUTHOR

Amy Dupire is a novelist and short story writer who grew up on a
steady diet of *The Twilight Zone* and *Alfred Hitchcock Presents*—in
rerun, of course

Made in the USA
San Bernardino, CA
29 July 2014